All We Are Given

Second Edition

WILL CROWTHER

ISBN: 978-1-7351040-0-3

DEDICATION

This novel is dedicated to my loving parents. My father came into a simple corner of this world – the U. S. West of 1896. He loved the nature around him. He taught that love to me, along with a desire for an education. Something he hadn't a chance to get himself.

Dad saw the Wright Brothers demonstrate their Flyer. Mom was a teen during the Roaring 1920s. She did get to complete public school. They lived through the Great Depression. They married after each had lost a spouse to death.

Dad founded a needed medical supply firm that survived him to become a multi-state corporation. My mom's continued love and support made it possible for me to follow my dreams.

Do not let the times discourage you. They will change. You will have great days along with the hard ones. "Be bold and mighty forces will come to your aid." Never stop dreaming.
Ad Astra!

CONTENTS

Acknowledgments ix

Prologue xi

Book 1 Double Down 1

1 We the People 3

2 The State of the State 5

3 Domestic Tranquility 9

4 Manifest Destiny 12

Book 2 It's Out There 15

5 The Other Side 17

6 The General Welfare 21

Book 3 Roads Less Traveled 23

7 The Rockets' Red Glare 25

8 Art and Possibility 32

9 The Party 37

Book 4 The Economy, Stupid 45

10 Proudly We Hail 47

11 The Only Superpower 51

Book 5 Tolerance and In-Toleration 57

12 All in the Family 59

13 Under God 63

14	Home Alone	66
Book 6	High Ground and Revelation	71
15	Brothers	73
16	All They Can Be	77
17	Greetings	83
18	Home for the Holidays	87
Book 7	Art of War	95
19	War Prayers	97
20	The Pursuit of Happiness	106
21	From on High	109
22	Motherland	112
23	The Children's Crusades	114
Book 8	Bob, Weave, and Conform	123
24	The Probe	125
25	Marching as to War	133
Book 9	Those Bastards	141
26	The Lion and the Lamb	143
27	The One(s) Too Many	149
28	Us Bastards	154
Book 10	Not Us	157
29	At the Crossroads	159

30	Kid Gloves	161
31	The Dark Side	165
Book 11	Coming Home	169
32	All Together Now	171
33	Getting Straight	174
34	Through a Looking Glass	177
Book 12	Surprise, Surprise	183
35	A Mouse Roars	185
36	Strange Love	187
37	Stalemate	190
38	All We Are Given	193
Book 13	The End	197
39	Of Future's Past	199
40	The Gulag	202
41	A Lighter Shade	204
42	Leap of Faith	206

ACKNOWLEDGMENTS

I thank my beta readers for their many good suggestions and corrections to early versions of this manuscript. And I thank them especially for their time and encouragement.

Cover: cwcdesign & engineering

Cover artwork by Dennis Mecham

ALL WE ARE GIVEN

THE ONLY IMPORTANT JOURNEY

The most humbling moment in life is seeing your child born. A father is a peripheral performer at this event. He is there to experience the wonder. Some males aren't even amazed. The experience passes overhead swiftly and the journey begins.

The life forms on this orb are so codependent that there must have been a master plan. Even the individual cells of higher organisms may be collaborations. Simple chance producing such synergies defies belief. And life's disregard of the physical law of increasing randomness hints at something outside physics.

Creation is so convoluted – even chaotic – that there can't have been a god. Random collisions of matter's smallest particles just might explain the cosmos. Yet each finite miracle like a child, a warm affectionate little dog, or a delicate rose with its thorns is so coherent and unique that a designer's hand seems reasonable.

What is important? What is knowledge? History is a fabric of distortions and lies. Disregarding history is ignorance. What do you pass to a child beyond a packet of genetic code? How do you nurture the unknowable future and instill in a child the hopes of their species? This is the big question. And the child is the only important journey.

For the destinies of our children and of their children: may the future happen for them in all the ways we wanted in our hearts but could not agree to in our times.

"Imagine all the people living life in peace."

ALL WE ARE GIVEN

BOOK 1

Double Down

ALL WE ARE GIVEN

1 WE THE PEOPLE

The history of the dominant species on the small blue planet is short but interesting. People evolved from this world's life stuff in ways similar to other species, and in ways distinct. Their clans grew into primal societies, tribes. Then they grew into larger feudal systems. Savage reign was common. But people did try a few social experiments. The journey from passive social existence to personal involvement took a long time.

Democracy came into being with literacy and the published stories of personal experience. The newly aware masses overthrew princes of power. Or they forced them to cede authority to favorites of the people. Politics separable from the sword was born. Marketing followed as night's gloom follows the day's clarity. Those freed gravitated to government by all the people.

Democratic city-states were born and flourished. Scientific progress and artistic freedom grew. Finally, people founded nations based on these ideas. The Princes who remain are largely ceremonial. Some say we could overcome mistrust and old prejudices now. With a planet-wide system of government where all men and women are equal; there are no Princes; and people live in harmony with each other and their world. Just Imagine.

Across the void of space and revolving around the same star another world teems with life. Intelligence arose there too. Personal awareness emerged. But personality dominated it among these creatures. The cult of Princely personality drives their superstitions. It defines their gods and shapes their societies.

Micah is a busy young man. He works hard at his classes, helps cover his tuition by working when he can, and manages a bit of social life as well. He lives at his parents' home. This isn't unusual for someone his age who is attending graduate school. His mother is an Orator in the House of Representatives. His father is a technocrat in private business. Micah is set to do well.

The war between Micah Daegan's country and the group of much smaller nations halfway around the globe has been going on for years. Many people paint the war to be about freedom and individual rights. Some say it's really about resources and access to them. Officially the war has much to do with safety and Security at home. Some even say gods are involved. References to ancient religious contentions and histories are often in the news.

Micah is safe from Forced Sacrifice for now. He has an Exemption. He maintains that by taking acceptable classes and earning satisfactory marks in school. 'Forcedsac', as people call it, was recently reinstated. It assures that there are enough soldiers to wage the expanding war. The war against ever larger foes in the block of countries that threaten Security and freedom and access to resources. Micah sometimes thinks about what could happen at the end of his studies, and of his Exemption.

Micah knows that he lives a life of privilege. His friends are similarly situated. Nearly everyone he has come to know while growing up is now in one highly desirable and very expensive school or another. Nearly everyone in Micah's exclusive school is descended from wealth and power.

"And we are all postponing the inevitable," thinks Micah. "We are all positioning ourselves for possible greatness."

2 THE STATE OF THE STATE

On a brisk Cold Season day Micah strolls into the Student Building. His first class is an hour off. He has time to drink a cup with some friends. And time to talk about the social scene, politics, and even some course work not fully understood. These times are important to Micah. Nearly all of his friendships revolve around school. Politics are fashionable to debate. But meeting the opposite sex and arranging social events are more important. Micah finds his friends' table and sits down to see what's up.

A spirited discussion over the coming nationwide elections is underway. So are arrangements for a weekend party featuring liquor and a lack of sober supervision. Micah is more interested in the party. He has already prepared for his Final Exams. The weekend is ripe for celebration or, if needed, mindless distraction from failure.

Lovely Raven is at the table. She has awed Micah since their first meeting a year ago. She is a transfer student from another school. She's intelligent, beautifully tall and willowy, and as smoky dark as her name. Fair-haired Micah is taller than her, but not by much.

Micah knows that Raven's father also sits in the House, on the Other Side from his mother's Party. He listens to find out if Raven will attend the end of school party at Gregory's house. Micah is looking forward to his final graduate school year with few cares. Discounting that annoying war on the other side of the world.

The argument over the election centers on support for the national Leadership in time of war. This is a midlevel election. The voters are choosing States' leaders. And they're choosing Representatives to the national Legislature. But top-level national Leaders are not up for election this time. Still, the arguments all involve preserving, or not, support for the Leadership and for the war.

Some wave patriotism as the only consideration during a war. Either you are a patriot and support candidates of the Leadership's Party. Or you are with the enemy. Some people consider the laws being upheld and public services being delivered to be irrelevant.

"Forced Sacrifice to fuel the war is wrong. It excludes the well placed, and ensnares people of good faith who oppose war on principle," says Gregory.

"Only people on the Other Side from the Leadership make these arguments," thinks Micah.

Micah learns Raven is coming to Gregory's party. He finishes his drink. He only smiles when asked to pick a side in the political debate. So does Raven. Micah picks up his things to go to his first course.

"Good luck on Finals everyone," Micah says as he leaves the Student Building to walk to class.

In the Capitol Complex, on the other side of the beautiful and formally arrayed city, the triumvirate is not happy. The three males, the Leadership; chosen initially seven years ago in a highly contested and some say questionable election; are tired of people second guessing their decisions at a time like this.

"The media have gone too far. Something has to be done to rein in their excesses," says the Prime Minister.

The PM is a belligerent person. He has little time or compassion for anyone in his way. The Secretary of Security and War is a soldier, up from the ranks. He has never married, has no children, and understands little of civilian life. The President just wants to enjoy his position. He's glad to let the other two decide real issues. While he plays for the media and performs ceremonial functions in grand style. However, he is angry now, along with the other two.

"This problem interferes with the parades of statesmanship. It makes overseas travel and visits here from foreign heads of state more difficult," says the President. "Questioning the record of the runup to war at a time like this – wartime – is unthinkable! The war has begun. The reasons for that are now moot. Only the efficient waging of the war is a proper topic for public discussion. And the 'loyal opposition' – the Other Side in the Legislature – is no better than the media."

All three men believe that the media and the opposition are working together. They are trying to bring irrelevant questions of fact before the people.

"Screws can be put to the media. And we can remind the people of their place," says the PM.

He and the Secretary have plans for a new Patrician Act to menace both.

Representative and Orator Jeannette Daegan, Micah's mother, is at home. She is preparing for talks in the House Chambers on a matter dear to her heart. Jenny, as her family and close friends call her, chairs the National Space Exploration Committee or NSEA. Funding for 'the Agency' in general and for its exploration of Near Planets and Celestial Objects, NPCO, is up for review. As it is every two years.

The President has called for a new space Initiative. It will involve impressive, if far in the future, crewed missions of exploration. Jenny Daegan will be responsible for coaxing the government to commit to funding the initial studies to begin to realize those dreams. Only follow through for years and even decades can bring such projects to fruition. Jenny is one of only a few people in the Federal Government capable of such long-term dedication.

"These missions are so far in the future that the President will be long gone from public service then. He will be gone before the hardware development costs are even met," thinks Jenny.

It is an exciting time for NSEA. The robot mission to the world's sister planet is nearing launch. The sister planet rotates in synchronization with home, but on the other side of the sun. Jenny saved the funding for this project from the axe of the Leadership's Economic Stabilization Program or ESP.

"Much larger savings can be had from social programs cuts, rather than from NSEA's tiny budget," she argued. The money saved will fund the next big round of Corporate Tax Reductions for Competitiveness.

CTRC is an ESP Initiative "— to restore balance in the private sector. And to ensure success for the nation in the world economy."

3 DOMESTIC TRANQUILITY

Gregory Kinkade is an exception at Micah's exclusive Upper School. Unlike Micah and most of the young adults attending there, Gregory is not wealthy or connected to power and fame. Gregory is an undergraduate on a scholarship. He attained admission to Upper School through sheer effort at his Lower School: magnificent grades. And through his parents' untiring and finally successful efforts to find a scholarship to help pay his way.

Young Mr. Kinkade also uses National Defense Student Loans to help fund his schooling. His two part time jobs are the final element allowing him to be the first Kinkade ever to go to Upper School. Gregory is always tired, exhausted even, by his labors. But he believes he knows his destiny. And he is on his own path.

It's not that the Kinkades are poor. Both parents work hard to maintain their home. It is in a nearly fashionable section of an outlying suburb of the Capitol. A modest inheritance let them buy the place years ago, when costs were lower. Gregory's parents' purposes now, later in life, are seeing their three children become all that they can be. Gregory is their oldest. For now, as he nears graduation, he is their center of the universe.

Micah Daegan is moving to his final year in graduate school. Gregory Kinkade is completing his final year as an undergraduate. Gregory has thought long and hard about graduate school. But he believes he can't afford that final finishing element without shorting one or both of his siblings' futures.

"Achieving something for every child – Upper School graduation – is the most important thing," thinks Gregory.

The Kinkades are happy to host a party, a coming out of sorts, for their oldest son as his graduation nears. Gregory is popular at school. Mr. and Mrs. Kinkade know that many who come to this party will be sons and daughters of important people. They urge Gregory to invite some of his cousins and even nieces and nephews of sufficient age.

"Impressions of success can be powerful goads. Sometimes great things 'rub off' on less well-situated people. And," his father says, "valuable contacts can be made at the least."

Gregory has convinced his parents that the party will not require their presence.

"These will all be well behaved young adults. I will see that property is not damaged; Enforcement Agents are not called; and that everyone gets home safely," he told them.

The argument in the Student Building reminded Gregory that he could soon face a real roadblock. He will reach a potentially fatal detour in life. One that could prevent his becoming a respected, educated, and well paid technocrat. His Exemption from forcedsac is about to end.

"Not everyone who is Available gets Chosen," thinks Gregory. No one he talks to knows how the choices are made. Gregory will just have to take his chances along with everyone else lacking an Exemption.

Greggy, as his close friends call him, puts thoughts of his party and of forcedsac out of his mind. He hurries from the Student building to the first of his very last Final Examinations.

"All of this; the party, exams, Upper School classes, and years of preparing for a better life; will be over by the end of the week," he thinks. He will soon be triumphant, and he is already a bit scared.

Greggy has relatives and Lower School friends who live in areas surrounding the vast city. Some of these are in adjacent states. Greggy has invited a few relatives near his age to the party. But few have promised to come. Some of the cousins that he invited live outside the social distances they can afford to travel. For some, those distances are only across the width of the sprawling city.

Raven Winthrop is an exception to this upper school's status quo too. It's not that her parents don't have money. They do. Her father's position on the Other Side from the current Leadership is a powerful one. It is much more powerful than Jenny Daegan's post. Raven's exception, her peculiar "disability" as her father puts it, is her chosen path in school. Raven is an Arts and Letters major. She, like Gregory, is about to graduate. Raven transferred from an even more prestigious school to this one. She did it to study with this school's world renowned art faculty.

Representative Markus Winthrop, Esquire, worries about his wayward youngest child's now approaching adulthood.

"There are no real advantages in Arts and Letters at all," Markus grumbles to himself. "An artist today needs luck and lots of it to achieve any measure of success that one could recognize." Though his Side in the House argues for funding for the arts in the public sphere; Markus does so for the Party instead of conviction.

"A graduate degree in the same field will be no help either," he says out loud. "Raven must be told the facts of life. Marry position or prepare for real toil at something responsible people value. And for that there is still time – in graduate school," Markus thinks.

Raven knows that she will lose her Exemption at graduation without a secured spot in a graduate program. Still, it seems to her that females are Chosen by forcedsac much less often than males. Even if she does not go on to graduate school; Raven's chances of dying far from home are significantly lower than, say, Gregory's.

4 MANIFEST DESTINY

Dr. Mariam Baker is excited. She's keenly aware of every detail that she sees. Mariam is anxiously awaiting the most important space launch of her career.

Dr. Baker has been the mind behind NSEA's Near Planets and Celestial Objects exploration programs for most of her professional life. She gave the approval to launch the first robot ships toward the moons. Dr. Baker called for the thumbs up from each Control Station before she let the first crewed vehicles launch into suborbital and then orbital flights. She pressed the launch sequence activation start button herself. Dr. Mariam Baker, Space Launch Facility One's Launch Director, is a legend in her own time.

Mariam has watched this latest countdown intently. The countdown weeks, which became days, have finally become mere hours. There were countdown holds. Problems have, most of the time, turned out to be faulty sensors rather than malfunctioning space hardware. Some problems have seemed to defy understanding. Mariam's tack in these cases is simple. Replace the whole damn system one element at a time, if necessary. Until all the boards light up green.

Dr. Baker knows Representative Jeannette Daegan well. She knows her both as a friend and a colleague. They are long distance friends to be sure. Space Launch Facility One stands on an island at the farthest south point of the nation. Nearer to the equator is easiest – less energy consuming – for a launch that wants to escape the planet's gravity well.

Dr. Baker and her husband live on the mainland across the narrow channel from the island. Theirs is a modest home in a beautiful location. Dr. Baker's work is her life and her reward is her work. Mariam truly loves what she gets out of bed every day for.

Dr. Baker's and Representative Daegan's paths cross often. Both in the north at the Capitol and at the launch facility. Jenny is a regular visitor to Space Launch Complex One. She comes to fact find in preparation for her speeches in the House in support of the work accomplished by the NPCO programs. Dr. Baker makes many trips to the Capitol to testify to the Representatives. Mariam expects to see Jenny at the launch tomorrow. That is if all goes well in the last hours of the countdown.

Astronomers knew for over a century that something was unaccounted for in their solar system. Modern celestial mechanics are quite precise. There is an unexplained change in the orbit of the planet next out from the home world. The change occurs as that planet passes near and then behind the sun. A similar but smaller change is seen in still farther out planets' courses.

To account for this, sixty years ago, they proposed an unseen 'sister planet'. This planet travels at the same angular speed and about one hundred and eighty degrees around the sun from the home world. Scientists debated the likelihood of such a thing for decades. They considered other explanations for the planets' paths. But those were all found wanting.

A sister planet on the opposite side of the sun most simply explains the orbits. And simple is almost always the way of nature. The planet might be somewhat smaller or somewhat larger than the home world. This depends on its distance from the sun and its orbit's declination from the ecliptic plane. The 'deltas'; the differences between the two planets in distance from the sun, orbital angle relative to the plane in which most of the planets rotate, and size; must all be quite small.

Probes sent to examine objects farther out in the system finally spied the sister planet. These probes were designed to explore specific visible targets. They turned them only briefly to look back a great distance at a posited one.

Observations made so far are shallow and imprecise. The planet exists pretty much as expected. It is no less than two-thirds of, and no more than one-third again, the size of the home world. Now, finally, a mission designed to explore the sister planet is ready to launch.

The design of the ship and its mission is based on the simplest, quickest way to get where it needs to go. Launch back – opposite the direction of rotation of the home world around the sun – and wait for the ship to run into the target. Or for the target to run into the ship. All things being relative.

The robot ship will be out of communication behind the sun at the time of contact. Elaborate software, 'artificial intelligence' of a sort, will let the ship calculate its own course changes then. These will be based on the robot's best measurements of the real size, location, and orbit of the target.

To maximize returns from this expensive mission, the ship is an orbiter rather than just a fly-by surveyor. The robot will be out of sight and communication when it encounters the planet. So, the probe will utilize its electronic 'brain' to calculate the mechanics of orbit.

It will determine the required braking engine burns; the minimum required orbital altitude; and the maximum time the probe can spend in orbit before leaving for home. And have enough fuel left to make it back to communication range. To safeguard the information gleaned, the ship will transmit its data as soon as possible. It will then attain home world orbit, if it can.

Due to the many unknowns, full mission success is not likely. If the probe detects greater than expected difficulties, it can choose a fly-by mission to prevent total failure. These difficulties might be a short on-orbit time with a low probability of escape; a planet atmosphere too deep or too opaque for instruments to function well; or other nastiness.

Mariam recalls the debates, the complex trade-offs, and the new technologies that set the mission's design and the ship's hardware. And she worries again about her responsibilities in all of this. "I must get the package delivered to the right address and in good health," she thinks.

BOOK 2

It's Out There

ALL WE ARE GIVEN

5 THE OTHER SIDE

"Finally, it will be done," Ibrahim thought as he waited for word that the orbital insertion burn came off as planned.

"Now the real work begins, my friend," said Ronald as he passed through the break room on his way to the outside world and a ride home for the night. "If the 'bird' is healthy and near the right location, we can start tweaking its orbit and aligning it with the others on Monday. Then there's the software that must all be re-matched to account for this final link in the net. Have a good one."

Ronnie was out the door. And Ibrahim headed to the Mission Room. He wanted to verify this news one more time.

"It's been such a long and difficult road to this," Ibrahim thought as he walked down a stark and nearly interminable corridor. Ibrahim Starks, SDS Senior Project Manager, has spent ten years of his life on this job. He has coddled; coaxed; and, sometimes it seemed, virtually shoved all of the sixty-three SDS spacecraft into geosynchronous orbit. They orbit above one of the two true space faring nations on the globe.

The nation lies north of the equator; so, the ships can't be truly geosynchronous. But they are at geosynchronous altitude. That's about thirty-five thousand eight hundred kilometres above the planet's surface. There they orbit at the same speed the planet rotates on its axis.

"Only satellites in orbits up to fifteen degrees north or south of the equator are in the so-called 'geostationary belt'," thinks Ibrahim. "Getting the 'birds' to behave so far north of the equator involves some delicate celestial mechanics. The trick was in timing each launch to make use of the positions of the moon and sun. All the while considering the final location or 'station' of each bird.

"Both the moon's and the sun's gravity affect the satellites. We used their positions in the sky at each launch to help us achieve a nearly geosynchronous condition for every bird. The sun and moon help us to maintain those stations too."

Ibrahim knows that the birds' stations do change slightly over time. But the satellites have station-keeping thrusters. And with them, the spread out 'net' of satellites can remain almost unchanged for years. While consuming only a small amount of onboard fuel.

The net of satellites sits in space above the nation. From the ground the net appears to oscillate a bit north and then back south every day. Each spacecraft traces out something like a figure eight in the sky. A geosynchronous satellite is one that orbits directly above the equator. It sits still above a single spot on the ground. It is geostationary.

Only fifty-seven of the birds complete the net. The other six are spares. They are supposed to swing into action if active birds fail at critical times.

Space Command paid to build and launch sixty-eight of the controversial spacecraft. Five of them failed to achieve orbit. They fell into the sea. The nation spent hundreds of millions of dollars trying to recover the Super Top Secret remains. Only a few hundred people including Ibrahim know that the satellites represent less than one third of the cost of the deployed system. Ibrahim does not have a 'need to know' what the astronomical development costs expended prior to fielding the hardware were.

"It looks good," says someone in the dark as Ibrahim enters the large room. Backlit control consoles fill this room. Its general lighting is minimal.

"Thank God for that," replies Ibrahim. "If my grandchildren's children are still going to be paying the bills for this, I want to give them a functional system for their money."

Ibrahim considers these words as they come out of his mouth.

"We'll have done well if any of these machines can find the broad side of a barn," he thinks. Ibrahim knows that they minimized real world testing to hold down costs. Many hardware and firmware revisions occurred during the ships' deployments. They can upgrade only a few of those. Some of the first fielded spacecraft will never work as intended.

There is an Initiative to swap some of the worst birds with some of the better spares. But the money and precious on-orbit fuel to move the hardware and rematch the software makes this less than likely. The system's costs are already far over projections. The budget overrun is under fire from all sorts of national interest groups. And swapping would make a mockery of the spares concept in the mind of anyone with a brain. Politics will probably kill any significant improvements in the space based portion of the system.

The Strategic Defense System, SDS, is the brainchild of a former Commander in Chief. He is long gone from that post. He dreamed of making his nation invulnerable to Intercontinental Missiles. Missiles that the other space faring nation on the planet possesses. It has taken over twenty-five years from imagining to deployment. But now one nation is on the verge of becoming 'the only superpower' in the universe.

The only superpower has ignored or reinterpreted long-standing treaties in order to field the clearly illegal system. The 'other side' has focused on both political and military countermeasures.

"The system is outdated before it is complete," a high official from that other side has smugly said. "The cost of building it will bury the aggressors."

Several consecutive Chief Executives bent to their Party's demand that they 'Sell deployment as if it is war'! Partly due to the system's cost, the nation's financial condition is at the lowest ebb it has seen in half a century. The dreamer's Party has held the balance of elected political power; either the Commander in Chief's post, voting control of the Legislature, or both; for all of the years required for the system's development and deployment. SDS was at least partly responsible for this too.

Party theorists and backers worried about losing the leverage the system represents with voters. So, they purposely slowed deployment. That cost the nation tens of billions of dollars more. It didn't improve the system at all.

SDS has driven the nation into an economic chasm. That chasm has begun to resonate with voter displeasure. Shrunken opposition parties are beginning to change people's minds. They're signing up voters at rates that alarm the men used to having their way all these years.

The moguls of the firms that benefited from the enormous and often noncompetitive contracts for the system are worried. These are the men in control of the ruling Party. And they're searching for a strategy to hold power.

6 THE GENERAL WELFARE

"Remember the boom after the World War. We were flying high inventing and building everything under the sun to satisfy our exploding population," says Howard. "We had the damned evil empire to prepare to fight in the Next Big War. We've got away from that 'war economy' that served us so well all those years. We need to get back to it."

"That's off the mark," replies Michael S. He is one of the ruling Party's biggest fundraisers, strategists, and a member of the National Steering Committee. "Times were different. What generated wealth for us then was our own consumption and the vast number of good jobs it created. We were feeding ourselves. Now our consumers consume stuff made and grown overseas. Only our weapons plants bring in solid dollars for us today. Thank God we're now the largest weapons dealers on the planet."

"But — SDS hasn't built up our economy. It has nearly broken it," someone in the back of the large conference room chimes in.

"That's because we're both the maker and the customer for SDS," Michael S. replies. "The money is going to the Corporations. Not that that's a bad thing. But it's taking its toll on the people's disposable income. We've created jobs here, but the numbers are small. We've saved money by overseas sourcing of routine small parts, documentation, and everything else we could. That's not a bad thing. After all, 'it's just another form of trade'."

"What we need is a war." Everyone turns to find the source of this simple declaration.

BOOK 3

Roads Less Traveled

7 THE ROCKETS' RED GLARE

"Hurry, Frank. Take the Main Street bridge," says Mariam to her driver. Dr. Baker is on her way to the airport to be the first to welcome Representative Daegan. The launch is only a couple of hours away now. Normally Mariam wouldn't leave the Control Room this close to a liftoff. But Jenny's visit might be as important as the launch this time. Mariam has decided at the last minute to go meet Jenny's plane. There are rumors afoot.

The whispered rumors say that after this project, the Leadership's Economic Stabilization Program Office plans to take another hard look at NSEA's budget. The probe to the hidden sister planet is probably the capstone of Mariam's career. But she knows that lack of money in the coming years will strangle other important journeys of exploration and discovery. Unless they can maintain the Agency's and its NPCO programs' funding.

"What is the Leadership thinking? The President's own crewed space Initiative might wind up on the chopping block," thinks Mariam. NSEA's budget is just over one percent of the nation's total budget. Savings here would amount to a drop in the bucket. Compared to the stated need to improve the bottom lines of the nation's major corporations. "Damn all those CEOs' hundred million dollar bonuses," thinks the Launch Director.

Representative Daegan has been composing her opening remarks for the coming NSEA Review. It will take place in the House of Representatives Auditorium. She is comfortable working in the small but luxurious government jet. It is made available for Representatives' junkets around the country. But Jenny doesn't like flying much.

"I'll be glad to be back on the ground," she says to herself. "And it will be good to see Mariam again." Jenny's mothering instinct interrupts her train of thought. "I hope Micah's test went well today."

Jenny knows that Micah has two more Finals tomorrow. And that he is going to Gregory's party after those. She hopes that doesn't get in the way of his studying for his last Final Examinations next week.

"He works so hard. I hope he doesn't let down until this school year is finished."

Jenny is glad she'll be at home for the weekend.

"I can help him stay focused on those last exams," she thinks. Jenny's position and reputation are important to her. But her loved ones' well-being and happiness are her greatest source of pride and joy.

Micah is in a great mood. His classes are all done. He has just passed his first Final with flying colors. He will have two of the remaining four exams done tomorrow. And tomorrow night is Greggy's party. Graduate students will have some exams next week. But the undergraduates coming to the party will already know their probable fates. They will be ready to celebrate or to drown their sorrows. And the lovely Raven will be there celebrating, or drowning and in need of comfort.

Micah drives home in the little red roadster his parents bought him for finishing his undergraduate degree. He plans tonight's reviews for tomorrow's Finals in his head.

Gregory arrived home tired but pleased with his day of Finals.

"Just two exams tomorrow and I will be finished forever," he thought. He ceremoniously removed the notes for the classes he finished today from his binder and put them in the trash. "Sure enough, someday I'll wish I hadn't tossed those. At least I've saved my most important books for future reference."

"What are we going to do about the ESP budget cuts?" Mariam asks Jenny. Mariam has dismissed her own car. She is riding back to the launch facility in Representative Daegan's limousine. So that they can have an uninterrupted conversation.

Jenny doesn't want to dismiss the rumblings Mariam speaks of as just rumors. She knows some of the people Mariam says are doing the whispering. These people should know better than to whisper if there isn't anything there.

"Well," says Jenny, "I'll focus my speeches on the facts that matter. I'll talk about how small a part of the federal budget NSEA gets. I'll explain how that money has benefitted us all. And I'll drive home the fact that the space budget has become very lean over the last several years. There's nothing left to cut without gutting entire programs.

"We'll talk more about this later, after this amazing probe of yours is on its way to whatever is out there, Mariam. Now you should concentrate on your launch. I'll gather impressions and build arguments. While I get to see another great Agency first."

Dr. Baker left launch central to meet Representative Daegan's airplane because she knew the most difficult milestones on the countdown had already passed. There is likely nothing to do now, at 'T minus one hour and thirteen minutes', except watch the clock run off the time.

People smile and shake hands with dignitaries. They discuss details with NSEA higher ups who have come out for the exposure. And they bathe in the mounting tension.

"It's like waiting for a date to pick you up for the prom. Or for the curtain to rise on an anticipated new play or opera in town," thinks Mariam. "Many preparations have been made. They have been checked again and again to make sure that things are just right. And everyone is expecting a wonderful time."

Just over an hour later; after lots of small talk, some minor countdown hiccups, and many congratulatory stops by the 'brass'; all attention turns to the big clock and the front wall video monitors showing the launch platform. Then all hell breaks loose.

"An unauthorized vehicle has entered the north launch platform gate. Shots! Umm — shots have been fired! Attention —" crackles a speaker somewhere in the back of the large room. The crowd had come to a hush before this. Everyone is staring at the monitors. They're waiting for the liftoff. They couldn't hear the voice on the little speaker otherwise.

"T minus fifteen seconds," says a louder voice coming from the big speakers up front. "Auto-ignition of main engines." Dr.

Mariam Baker, a living legend, has just finished surveying her Systems Control managers. All the lights are green. Dr. Baker flips up the clear cover over the bright red Final Ignition Sequence Start button. She exposes the last hurdle to lighting the fires that will send the bird flying.

"Explosion — there has been an explosion at the north platform gate!" comes the voice from the small speaker. The main speakers broadcast the low hiss of the vehicle's core, liquid fueled rocket engines.

"T minus ten seconds." People in the Control Room are moving now. They're responding to the fact that something horribly unexpected is going on. Dr. Baker processes several seemingly unrelated facts in her head.

"The North gate is one and a half kilometres, nearly a mile, from the launch platform. It has no access to anything launch related. — It's time to ignite the solid fueled strap-on booster motors that provide most of the thrust for liftoff of this heavy rocket. — This mission may be the last one before the ESP and CTRC effectively shut down scientific progress."

"T minus five seconds." NSEA's legendary Launch Director, Mariam, slams her palm down on the big bright red button. Almost instantly they hear the roar, a kind of continuous explosion, of the six powerful boosters. It's heard first over the main speakers and then through the building's walls. The energy being unleashed on that heavy concrete pad nearly two kilometres away makes the floor of this vast building tremble. Launch Director Baker realizes that all eyes in the room are turning to her.

Representative Markus Winthrop, Esquire, sits waiting for his daughter to come home. He doesn't know that Raven will be home soon. It isn't as if she promised to be home. Her parents don't keep close reign on an independent adult like twenty-two year old Raven. Still, there is a good chance she will be home shortly.

Markus knows that Raven's classes are over for the day, but that she must sit for more Examinations tomorrow. Markus is home from the Capitol Complex earlier than usual. He has decided that now is the time to have that discussion with Raven.

While he waits, Markus idly watches the early evening news. He changes channels several times, looking for some college sports scores. Markus never played sports, at any level, but he sometimes follows his alma mater's teams just for the fun of it. They interrupt the local weather for a Bulletin. Some voice says something about a problem at the Space Launch Complex.

"Easily fixed," Markus thinks. He changes channels once again. "Damn," he swears under his breath, "it's on this channel too. It's probably on all of them now. Better have a listen then."

There has been an apparent terrorist attack at the launch complex. No one is known to be hurt except for the attackers. Their vehicle rammed a gate and then blew up as it sped off inside the complex. Why or how the vehicle exploded is unknown at this time. How many attackers were involved is also unknown.

Damage to the facility, if any, is undetermined.

"Stay tuned for further information," it says on a ticker at the bottom of the screen. The picture reverts to the College Sports Roundup.

"I forgot that big space launch to the other side of the sun was today," thinks Markus. He glances down the hall at the door to the garage again. He settles his large frame more comfortably in the big chair. "Let's see if we've won at sculls again. I hope Raven gets home before her mother. So that we two can chat about this decision without any argument."

They quietly hustle Mariam Baker to a conference room out of sight of the pandemonium in the Control Room. The Security men who escort her idolize the diminutive 'Dr. Mariam'. But they move now with grim urgency. The 'big brass' they usually do their best to avoid have given them direct orders.

Dr. Baker's superiors, who were out to bask in the glow of the media and dignitaries at the launch, appear shaken. They assemble one by one in the room. As many people as can, sit down at the conference table. The rest stand lining the walls. They leave Mariam on her feet alone at the front of the room.

"Why in the hell did you launch?" asks some voice. Mariam is watching the single video monitor in this room intently. She doesn't turn to identify the source of this interruption.

"I kept my head and followed the mission, Sir," she responds blankly. The launch looks good. All the telemetry readings, which are ripping across the bottom of the screen on a ticker, are nominal.

"But — we are under attack!" says the voice.

"We were under attack, I believe," Mariam says.

"Booster separation completed" comes from the little speaker on the monitor.

"The bird could be damaged. It might have been sabotaged!"

"The bird is healthy," says Mariam. She breaks from the screen to scan the faces around her as she points to the monitor. "I've followed every detail for days," she says to Sam Chakroborty, the Program Manager for this shot. Sam is not Mariam's superior, but she reports to him and he consults with her on this mission. Sam is standing against the back wall of the room.

"Whatever happened, happened well outside the range of any critical systems," she continues. "Launch had already begun. The liquid engines were firing. All the boards were green and it was time to commit."

"We can shut down liquid fueled engines, Mariam." Dr. Baker recognizes the voice making this last statement.

"Dr. Jacobsen, Sir," she replies, turning to face the seated Executive Director of Space Launch Complex One. "It was my call."

They removed visiting VIPs from the mission control building as quickly and gently as possible. With them went the big brass that make some of the room's regular denizens so nervous. Everything on the facility seems to be on normal status now. Except for the situation at the North gate. But reports from there are becoming calmer.

The intruders' vehicle that exploded and burned has been put out. They have secured the smashed gate to the satisfaction of the Chief of Security. It's all over except trying to figure out what the hell it was all about.

Representative Jeannette Daegan was asked to leave the Control Room along with the other visitors. But they did not remove her from the Launch Complex. Dr. Mariam's Assistant showed Jenny to the Launch Director's outer office. She offered her food, a choice of things to drink, and any services she might need to go on with her official duties. These include secretarial help and access to outside communication systems. Jenny went back to composing her opening oration and wondering when she could talk with Mariam about all the day's events.

"There's Raven now," thinks Markus when he hears a car in

the drive. His beautiful daughter, Raven Michelle, looks tired. "Final Exams," he recalls. "So much preparation and stress. Raven, let's you and I talk about your future. Can I make you a cup of tea and we'll sit in the breakfast nook?"

Markus knows that Raven loves the nook at night. She likes to study there. Where she can look out the many windows at the lighted gardens of their terraced back yard.

"Sure, Dad," Raven says. "What would you like to know?"

8 ART AND POSSIBILITY

Raven Michelle Winthrop isn't just an Arts and Letters major. Raven is a composer of classically inspired music. She's a painter of beautiful and evocative pictures. Several of Raven's paintings hang on the walls of her parents' home. Even Markus recognizes something very special in his daughter's work. In the 'disability' that keeps her from committing to any valuable occupation in his eyes.

"They're as beautiful as anything you can see on the walls at the capitol's Museum of Art," he tells visitors to the house as he shows them Raven's work. Virtually all of those visitors agree with his judgment. And given the Winthrops' social position, some of these people are likely to know.

In truth, Raven is a wonderful watercolorist. Her art professors stand in awe of her abilities. Though ego prevents most of them from saying that.

R. Michelle, as her music professors and fellow composition students know her, writes hauntingly beautiful music as well. Her paintings inspire her music and her music gives life to her paintings. If she's lucky, Raven Michelle could become one of the most acclaimed artists of her time. In this respect, Markus is right. Raven will need luck, as any artist through all of history has needed it.

Markus brews the orange pekoe and herbal tea his daughter loves. Raven sits in the half round breakfast nook with the lights turned down. This showcases the view of the beautiful, softly lighted gardens in the deepening twilight. Raven might not have gravitated to creating beauty if it hadn't surrounded her all her life.

Markus and his wife, Nancy, haven't done any of the landscaping or decorating of their home themselves. They hired the best landscape architects and interior designers for the work. The faithfully restored antique grand piano in the formal sitting room is decoration to the Winthrops. It has been inspiration to their daughter to take up the study of music.

"Dad, I've thought about graduate school – a lot, actually," begins Raven. She knows her father only too well. "My grades and especially my teacher's remarks and expressions – their faces – tell me I should just make my way, do my work, from here on.

"Did I tell you that my 'masterpiece' is hanging in the school's Arts Center Main Exhibit Hall? Daddy, I won the Senior Painting Competition. I actually won! It was just announced today, the winners that is."

The pen and ink, watercolor, and pastels work that won the annual painting competition for Raven Michelle is a large piece. It is almost two metres by just over a metre high. It tells a story, as do all of Raven's works. This one tells a literal story. Some of her paintings' narratives are allegorical. They expand on her musical compositions. Paintings that wistfully portray changing Seasons' rites are some of these.

Raven's masterpiece tells a story of hope. It is a story of reunion or of newfound harmony between two groups of people coming together in trust and fraternity.

"Raven, my dear," says Markus, "I'm not speaking of graduate school in terms of an Arts degree, but rather as a new challenge for you. I want to encourage you to pursue a field where you can be of service to your fellow beings.

"For generations now, Winthrops have served our nation's political and social systems. We have served in various capacities. Now that you have completed your undergraduate work, you should look beyond that. You should attain some real measure of distinction in service. Your new work should reflect that, Raven.

"You'll never want for money in this world. But I'd like to see you able to make your own way without relying on marriage or your family. I think a competent and independent woman today should be all of that.

"Of course, some day I would like to see you with a family of your own to nurture," continues Markus. "That too is one of life's duties and rich rewards. You should be cherished, my dear. Both by the public and by your own family. No one can do better than this: to contribute to his or her society in its time, and to each adoring family member. While standing as an example to all people."

Raven sips her tea for a moment, glancing about the serene gardens arrayed below them before speaking.

"Daddy, I agree with everything you've just said so beautifully about family and society. I believe my art can be a contribution to our country and to the whole world. To be an artist one must know in her deepest heart that her art is real, that it is important, and that it speaks to people's souls. This is what I want to do with my life. I want to contribute to people's awareness of higher purposes and goals beyond the workaday world.

"I want to show beauty to people who might otherwise be too absorbed in struggling to see it. I want what I do to inspire people's spirits to seek harmony and beauty, and to know compassion. I'm not going to graduate school, Dad."

"Daughter, this is not a good time to be without an Exemption to Forced Sacrifice. There are other ways to acquire an Exemption, but you are not prepared for any of them. Right now, the only way you can reliably protect your freedom and your very life, my dear, is by going to graduate school.

"You are an adult. I cannot force you to go to school. Still, I must for your sake bring certain pressures to bear. I must do everything I can to protect you, Raven. Even to protect you from yourself."

"Daddy – Markus, please let me show you something. Come with me to the tall room and let me tell you about my work."

"How can I not protect my little girl?" thinks Representative Winthrop as he follows Raven to see her paintings hanging in the entry foyer. "And how can I do what I'm contemplating to her, even for her own good."

Markus chuckles to himself at 'tall room'. It's a name Raven has used since she could first talk. It's her name for the formal entry with its two storey high ceiling, massive chandelier, and double sweeping staircases to the upper floor.

Raven stops near a small painting that hangs above a desk in the alcove beneath one of the stairs. The alabaster white walls; the fluted columns and pilasters that support the stairways; and the large, bias laid black and white marble tiles on the floor give this big room, actually just an entry hall, an approaching-stark formality. It is an art museum waiting to be given color and meaning by the works hung there.

The piece Raven points out, it seems to Markus, has always been in the family.

"I can't recall when we didn't have it." One of R. M. Winthrop's early Seasons watercolors, it's not large as many of her later works are. Raven consults the small house communications panel on one of the walls of the alcove. She pushes a few buttons. A piece of music she wrote a long time ago in her young life wafts through the big house.

"Daddy, I wrote this music to go with this painting." Markus is surprised. He loves this music. It reminds him of the approaching Cold Season. It makes him feel the cool air moving the changing leaves around. And, somehow, it reminds him of the crisp smells in the blustery atmosphere.

Markus is drawn closer to the painting. Yes, he remembers this well. It shows a dirt path through a small scrub forest. The overarching trees that close completely above the path are ablaze with leaves colored by the approaching Cold time. Already loosed leaves dance in the embrace of a little whirlwind at one side of the path.

The course passes directly away from where you stand. The shadows of the vegetation deepen upon it as it goes. One can almost believe the painting has real depth. Markus has stood here times before and walked this track in his mind.

Representative Winthrop knew vaguely that his daughter wrote music as well as making her pictures. He is suddenly aware of how little awareness he has shown.

They allowed all the contest winning art works at the Upper School to advertise as For Sale. The school leaves it up to the artists. This is not usually permitted in the school galleries. Raven, on a lark born of the euphoria of winning, added a note to her painting's title sign. She offered it at an astronomical figure.

"It's just a prank," she thought as she penciled in the number. "No one could think I'm serious." Raven isn't sure that she'd part with her masterpiece at any price. R. M. Winthrop may think the dollar value she has applied to her masterwork a joke. But there are some who would consider it a bargain at almost any price.

9 THE PARTY

Finally, it is done. The last undergraduate Final Exam has passed. Most students have nothing left to do but trudge home and summarily destroy their class notes. Or archive them for some unknown future purpose.

Some professors have scheduled, in spite of policy, a few undergraduate Final Exams on the weekend. Graduate students have some Finals scheduled next week. But otherwise the regular school year is over. The party weekend of the year is about to launch.

Gregory, Micah, Raven, and their crowd of loosely orbiting students are going to cut loose at the Kinkade home in the suburbs. They'll be joined by some of Greggy's kin.

Mrs. Kinkade has spent days cleaning the house and removing her most delicate possessions from harm's way. She and Gregory's father are leaving now for a night's stay at a nearby bed and breakfast. There they can enjoy some solitude. But they'll remain available in case anything goes wrong at home.

"It's good to have them out of here," thinks Gregory, as his parents pull out of the drive in the family car. "Now to unpack and stock the bar with the 'other' liquor. The stuff Dad doesn't know about."

Some of the graduating students coming for the night's fun have more than the end of school to celebrate. Some have new job offers to brag about. Jobs that will take them all over the country and even the world. In some cases, these jobs will provide them with continuing Exemption from military service.

More than a few new graduates are about to begin voluntary Enlistment. They do this to escape forcedsac. That would leave them with fewer training and other choices in military life. Some of these people are proud to volunteer to serve their country in time of war. Some believe they must take this course to avoid dying for ill defined purposes. In a conflict they consider immoral. And there are some, now Available for forcedsac, who are considering radical alternatives to military life.

Each newly minted soldier and his or her parents have been deeply involved in this decision. Most believe their choice to be best for the soldier, the family, and even for the nation. But some consider anyone weighing ideas other than submission to the will of the Leadership to be traitors. More than a few of these righteous souls consider having political opinions beyond party platform traitorous. They even think them to be blasphemous. As religion somehow enters the fray on the side of organized killing. And of course, only one party's positions are acceptable.

Gregory has staked out the entire basement including the wet bar, the living room and kitchen, and the covered patio and garden out back as party central. Two portable firepots on the patio will keep that space warm enough for fun even if the evening gets cold.

The bedrooms upstairs are not to be included. Greggy's younger brother and sister are to have free run of the second floor. They are not old enough for an adult party.

The guests begin arriving. Gregory turns on the communications system and cranks the volume to a happy, resonant level. He punches in several hours of what he hopes will be everyone's favorite music. Then he starts serving drinks in the basement.

"I'm glad everyone seems pleased with their Finals," Greggy thinks. "An unhappy drunk is potentially a belligerent drunk. I'm into everyone having a good time tonight: getting loose; enjoying friendly company, some of it very friendly; and not having to deal with much drama."

When Micah arrives, the party is blasting away. Parking out front in the dead-end court is at a premium. People are roaming all about the property, including the front yard.

"Partying on the public sidewalks is not a good plan," Micah thinks as he enters.

The music is having a hard time competing with an explosive level of laughter and sing along inside the house.

"It's going to be a great time," Micah says to himself. He orders his favorite drink in the basement from Greggy, who is still hanging behind the bar. Then he begins circulating through the house. He is on alert for the lovely and always amazing Raven.

Micah is well known and liked. He stops to engage in a little banter with each cluster of people who hail him. Most of the discussions he hears revolve around the Exams. "How did you do on O'Brien's Differential Equations Final?" "Do you think Smith will grade the International Relations exam on a curve?" And so on.

These are the hopeful future leaders of a nation. They've worked hard to position themselves for possible greatness. And they damn well want to know that some trick question on an exam isn't going to torpedo their dreams.

There is a lot of sexual swagger going on as well.

"People who are 'riding high' and feeling good about their futures will totally reveal themselves while propositioning the opposite sex," thinks Micah. "Especially when they're well lubricated." The party gets louder as Micah moves from the front to the back of the house. When he steps out onto the patio, he is amazed at the volume. "There are a lot of people here!"

The back yard is more of what's inside. People have staked out a dance floor on one end of the large patio. And they've turned up the backyard's speakers even louder than the ones in the house.

There are people all over the large garden. There are couples walking and talking privately. And knots of people laughing, bantering, and railing about this and that. At the outer edge of the patio, near the dancers, there is a loud argument going on where a large group has gathered.

Two of Gregory's cousins arrive at the address on their invitation. The party is large and loud. The neighbors are surveying it anxiously. Gregory's parents warned every house within screeching distance of the event. They begged every householder for their consent. They apologized in advance for any inconvenience caused. Still, the party seems larger and louder than many neighbors thought it would be. And people drinking on the public sidewalks is definitely too much.

The cousins are Kinkades and brothers. People who have done this too many times tonight shoo them from leaving their car blocking a driveway. The brothers finally park their older, dilapidated vehicle around a corner. It is just outside the court, away from the nearly new cars that pack the usually quiet neighborhood.

"These arguments are everywhere now," thinks Micah as he steps up to the crowd by the dancers. People about to trade college life for military discipline are arguing with those opposed to the war, forcedsac, and the Leadership's policies.

A particularly loud male, who Micah knows only as Dick, proclaims that his father, "a true patriot and veteran of war;" understands the need to fight the enemy "wherever, whenever, and however our leaders tell us to."

"Everyone else has met the call through our country's history. It's our duty to do the same," says a woman who proclaims her Enlistment proudly.

Several spectators who may or may not have joined up to serve nod in agreement. But one young man is nearly single handedly leading the charge against the war.

"That is Jimmy, I believe," thinks Micah. Jimmy is standing firmly against having to accept this war without question just because others have.

"Would you blindly jump from a cliff to die because some already have and a line is forming?" says the brave antagonist. "The sanity of a thing and the morality of a thing are not defined by whether it has already devoured some or been agreed to by others.

People at the edge of this crowd drift off and new ones arrive while the argument rages. Many of these students are trained in debating the merits of any position, including the status quo. But there are things to do tonight that provide more fun and provoke less sullen anger than this argument portends. Few join the battle on either side.

"My good friend!" says Greggy as he hands Micah, just in the dry nick of time, a fresh drink he's brought for the purpose. "I've turned the bar over to less-senior partners. I'm now rewarding the masses with my presence." Micah grins and then smiles more broadly as he sees Raven, lovely amazing Raven, approaching.

"Glad to see you made it," says Gregory to two younger looking men who stop to shake his hand. His cousins have found the bar and then the back yard. They have gravitated to the large concentration of females near the dance area. "Enjoy and I'll see you around," Greggy says as he resumes mingling for the first time this evening. He disappears back inside the house.

"Well, how were your Finals?" Micah asks Raven.

"I did well. I'm pretty sure. But something better than graduating happened to me, Micah. I won the senior painting contest."

"Congratulations Raven! Are you going to go on for a graduate degree in Art then?"

"No, Micah. I'm not. I'm going out into the world to be an artist, rather than studying being an artist."

"Then — how about your Exemption?" Micah asks.

Many heads in the knot of people arguing about the war and forcedsac turn their way. Micah's last words have fallen during a lull in the heated contest. People all around have heard him.

"Obviously, I'll be taking my chances at being Chosen if I'm Available," Raven says. She says it as much to the other people listening as to Micah.

"Hear, hear! Let's drink to the lady's courage," proclaims Dick. Micah and Raven, who have until now refused to join in arguments over the war, find themselves deep in the middle of one.

"Forced Sacrifice has been used in past wars to unfairly draft low income and less influential people to die. While the powerful just talk," says one of the young Kinkades. "My father told me what it was like. When forcedsac was used even during peacetime. I believe him."

"Anyone who argues against the war is a coward and a traitor," beats Dick.

"Regardless of whether the war is right or wrong, we should go back to an all volunteer military," says the other young Kinkade.

"That statement's naïve," thinks Micah. What Raven says next stuns him.

"If I'm Chosen, I'll flee the country or refuse forcedsac and face prison for my convictions. We all need to stand and be counted in the struggles against all wars and for freedom from oppression," she says.

"So, the lady isn't courageous after all. She's just a big talker and a traitor to the country that gives her so much freedom," says Dick. "You belong in prison for what you've just said. I'll see that the authorities know about your attitude."

Micah manages to turn Raven away from the core of arguing people.

"Be careful what you say in public," he whispers. "Right now, this is no longer 'The home of free men and brave'."

Raven is as surprised as Micah by what she has just revealed.

"I guess I've been thinking about this without consciously admitting how I feel," she says. "War and politics these days, like these arguments denying individual thought and demanding absolute fealty to the Leaders' personal positions —. Well, they're both opposed to the things I believe in. They're opposed to what I want my life and my work to stand for. And the words I just spoke. They're not even my words. I was quoting Greggy from that discussion in the Student building. I guess I admire Gregory for his willingness to stand up for what he believes in."

Micah is walking now. He's walking away from the rising shouts from Dick and the others like him: people standing in a line and at a crossroads. Raven is coming with Micah, hesitantly. They're going to the back door and the supposed sanctuary of the house. Suddenly, Agents burst through that door and begin fanning out among the guests in the backyard.

"Turn off that music! Everyone just stand where you are. Get away from the garden walls. Anyone with a drink is going to have to show us identification. Everyone needs to get his or her identification out where we can see it," yells the first Enforcement Agent through the door. "Where is the owner of this house, does anyone know?"

"Oh hell," whispers Micah, "some neighbor has called us in."

On the main floor of the Kinkade residence half a dozen Agents are examining people's papers. The music, both inside and out, goes silent. Gregory approaches an Agent wearing a coat and tie rather than a uniform.

"I'm the owner of this house. What do you need?"

"Let me see your identification. Are you aware that you're violating several domestic regulations? Those include serving liquor to the underage and commandeering a public roadway for private parking. And exceeding noise limits. Who owns that suspicious car parked out of sight around the far corner? Do you really own this home or are you just an underage resident? Where are your parents?"

While Gregory is explaining the situation to the Agent, the other Agents are examining papers. But they are failing to find anyone underage with a drink. In fact, they fail to find anyone below the age of majority inside the house, either on the main floor or in the basement. In the backyard however, Gregory's cousins admit to both being underage and to driving that suspicious car parked out of sight around the far corner.

They are arrested. As is a drunk calling himself 'Dick'. Dick has no ID. He waylays the senior Agent with a tale. One of "probable illegal activity and certainly illegal thought" by someone who might resist forcedsac at some later date.

The party comes to an ignoble but relatively benign end. The Agents, who were called out about a suspicious car, tell everyone to "Go home immediately or be arrested."

Micah finds himself driving the always amazing Raven home.

BOOK 4

The Economy, Stupid

ALL WE ARE GIVEN

10 PROUDLY WE HAIL

Ibrahim spent the next several weeks tweaking this and tweaking that. And reporting on all the tweaking to his higher ups. The final SDS spacecraft was about where it belonged and in good health. So, it was time to make the system work. This is largely a software thing.

Ibrahim is a component design engineer and a system engineer. He's not a computer scientist. He just tries to accurately pass on the status of re-matching the ground based and orbital units' software.

As Ibrahim understands it, every bird knows its own 'address' or station and the addresses of the other birds in its subnet zone. Birds at the perimeters of subnets must also know their subnet's master address in an overall net matrix. The few but important 'monument' spacecraft memorize the entire network relative to fixed ground emplacements; keep track of where the net is as it moves slightly north and south over the nation each day; and perform other critical functions.

Birds farther from the equator oscillate a greater distance north and south than the ones closer to it. The monuments must continuously account for these changes in the distances between birds. They adjust for longer term changes in the stations' locations too.

Ibrahim understands the net's changing geometries well enough. But when he tries to imagine the math required to precisely locate a moving target by triangulation with several birds; which are themselves moving over the surface of a sphere enclosing the planet at geosynchronous altitude; he gets lost.

"I'll just leave that part to the master mathematicians and the scientific programmers making the big money," Ibrahim thinks. And he does.

The monument ships also 'heal' problems that occur with space asset software, wherever that software is located. They can, sometimes, compensate for malfunctioning space hardware. And make the system work. The monuments are specialized. They are each designed for a specific station. The rest of the birds in the flock are interchangeable, in theory. They need only a software upload to move to a new location in the net.

Ibrahim found out when a monument failed to reach orbit that they cost more than the four billion dollar price of each regular bird. Apparently, they cost a lot more. Ibrahim knows less about the workings of the monuments. Enough less that he is unable to guess as to their 'achieved functionality'. There are no monument spares in orbit.

The Ruling Class; as some call the cabal at the core of the most powerful political Party of the only superpower in the universe; dragged their feet for years during fielding of the SDS hardware. They did this to stretch out the political advantage given to them by the system. But they quickly trumpeted completion of the satellite network. Ibrahim knew, even after the system had been in place for nearly two months, that the tweaking was incomplete. Nothing would work yet if it were called on.

For the system to work, the matching of spacecraft locations, bird-specific software, and ground based assets must all be virtually perfect. Then, the system can locate, track, and direct fire from space and from the ground to destroy the other side's Intercontinental Missiles in flight. At least, that's true in theory.

The saber rattling began when they announced that the SDS satellite net was complete. The other side calls it "The greatest provocation from the aggressors ever." Their Premiere repeats often that "The system is outdated and unworkable even now, when it is brand new." Also frequently heard is "We are prepared to meet the first strike intentions of the aggressors. Their foolish preparations to strike in the most cowardly way; at our cities, to kill millions of innocents; will be repelled and answered in blood."

Ibrahim charts the alignment and software matching of the space based assets for his presentations to the brass. Each presentation builds on the previous ones. The progress that they show closely matches the Master Schedule, most of the time. Ibrahim keeps more detailed charts for his own information.

"I can see where it's coming together," Ibrahim thinks. "The birds are beginning to respond as a unit; instead of acting as individual elements. They're becoming more and more like a flock of biological birds."

Ibrahim also sees where some of the earliest, least capable ships are holding the network back. They are creating holes. These are slow response points in the theoretically uniform and impenetrable shield. Computer coders work frantically to write software that compensates for faulty space firmware and hardware. Ibrahim sees to it that these software 'patches' are uploaded to the weak birds.

Ibrahim knows that he has an opposite number somewhere who is dealing with the ground based assets.

"Between us – I and 'Mr. X' – we know more about the system that exists, as opposed to the hypothetical one that never will exist, than any other two people alive." Ibrahim is right about that. And he isn't the only person to realize it.

The military's top officers create traction between well known, budget endowed politicians and the joint services. The government shields the services from the public. The military has only command structure and manpower. But these General Officers function at some level in both of these worlds. They get the military's weapons needs fielded. In the most complete form that money and politics will allow.

Generals rely on special subordinates to keep them informed as to the hardware and software they're really getting. High level Technical Specialists who get the big picture are important military assets.

Generals know that those same military specialists will not be around for long. Even 'lifers' who make the service their careers have their positions reshuffled often by the military. This creates the need for civilian Contractor specialists. The military can retain Contractors for the years or decades that major C3; Command,

Communications, and Control systems; and major weapons will be in the inventory.

SDS is the largest system the superpower has ever fielded. It's the most complex one too. Its expected lifetime is unknown, except to a few. It's assumed to be very long. Mr. Starks and 'Mr. X,' a Mr. Valentine, have lucked into lifelong job security, if they want it.

For Ibrahim the security comes as a promotion and a large salary increase. This coincides with the end, more or less, of the net's tweaking. Moving from Senior Project Manager to Director of the new Strategic Space Systems Division is a big step. For an engineer who thinks of himself as "just another grunt who gets the real work done."

So, with a big title and little money in the scheme of things, Ibrahim, 'company man', is secured; probably for life. He understands and accepts it all. Ibrahim Starks is looking forward to working with Neil Valentine. Neil is an engineer with 'those other guys'. He works for the rival firm that handled assembly and fielding of almost all of SDS's ground assets.

There is one program milestone left. One box still to check off before the original SDS contracts are complete. They have written and validated the system's Operations Manuals and Maintenance Manuals. They have trained and certified Military Technical Specialists to sit at the control consoles. The system has been formally, provisionally, turned over to SDS Command. And Contractor infrastructure for the long haul is in place. But there is still one final task to accomplish: the Operational Test.

The ground and space based components must demonstrate that they are in fine tune. Ibrahim's net of birds and Neil Valentine's C3 units and ground based weapons must show that they are one system. They must prove they can do what those Development and Performance Specifications written long ago by people no longer in the game say they can do. It's time to shoot something down.

11 THE ONLY SUPERPOWER

"Well, we finally have our impenetrable shield in place to protect us from Intercontinental Missiles," says Ronnie.

"Yes" says Ibrahim. "And one day it may even work."

The coworkers are eating lunch in the break room. They have been discussing the nearly complete tweaking of the SDS net's flock of orbiting spacecraft.

"I listened to a news story last night that said SDS will reduce the incentive for compromise with other nations. That the only superpower can now do just about whatever it wants," says Ronnie. "I don't think we will do that. But in my opinion, being there is good."

"The Ruling Class will focus on maintaining political power," says Ibrahim. "They have determined that, to maintain control in this new era, our tattered economy should be improved. It's past time that someone did that. We need to compete in the world again. We need to make things that people everywhere want to buy."

Many lesser but developed nations have more robust economies than the only superpower does now. Some of these are making and selling, growing and selling, and digging up and selling products and commodities to the superpower. And right now, they're doing this at the limits of their factories' and farms' and extractive industries' abilities.

One of the superpower's allies builds the bulk of the world's automobiles. They also design nearly all of the planet's electronic devices. Ibrahim's brother and sister-in-law work for one of that country's big corporations. They work in a factory not far from the only superpower's capitol. They assemble automobiles that people all over the world agree are the best. The corporations of the nation that designs the best cars do their final assembly in each of their major markets. This reduces overall costs. It allows them to better compete with these market's own automobile makers.

"My brother and his wife make good wages building cars. Better than they could in most non-manufacturing jobs. The company they work for is not one of ours. It just has some assembly plants here. They provide no long-term benefits to employees. We need our own corporations to get back to manufacturing on our own soil."

Ibrahim's brother and sister-in-law's health insurance is minimal. They have no pension plans. But that's where the superpower's own corporations are going anyway. Paying only wages to workers and avoiding long-term commitments helps lower the cost of the cars. Which also benefit from inexpensive transport to local dealers. The components that Ibrahim's relatives put into cars are nearly all produced in less developed countries. Labor there is very cheap.

"I enjoy visiting my brother," says Ibrahim. "I get to see the latest electronic games and gizmos that the company he works for makes. The company lets its employees buy them for ten percent off."

A group of nations raises or grows most of the materials used for clothing around the world. They sell finished apparel too. Together these countries are clothiers to the planet. But workers from less developed countries cut out and sew the clothes. They do this in the countries where the clothes will sell.

Sometimes these clothing 'sweat shops' in the superpower are raided. The wages they pay are below the scant minimum required by law. Management chains the workers to the sewing machines. The workers are often in the country illegally. When they are, they get deported.

A few nations have important natural resources in abundance beneath their feet. These nations support their populations and their rulers by parceling out access to these. They do it in a way that keeps the big powers from warring over them. And sees to it that everyone gets, if not what they want, at least what they need. These nations are far from poor. But control of access to resources keeps their rulers among the last real Princes on the globe.

"Too many people here are forced to accept a declining standard of living as they get older," says Ibrahim. "The government maintains this isn't so. But it passes new laws allowing corporations to keep more of the money they make by paying less tax. The Ruling Class says this corporate savings will 'trickle down' to average workers. But I see stagnant wages. And workers making up for corporations' reduced taxes by paying more tax themselves.

"The loss of national pride in taking care of our own is obvious. There are vanishing employee benefits, like health insurance and retirement plans. There are banking and tax changes that reduce the interest earned on employees' investments in our system. These changes hurt us all. But they especially hurt our seniors. They have invested in our nation all of their lives. And all of these things happen without protest from our government. From the government '— by, for, and of the people'."

"Some aboriginal groups' elders wander off to die when they are no longer useful," says Ronald.

"The global economy has grown. More nations are evolving," says Ibrahim. "Some countries we used to have large trade surpluses with we now have trade deficits with."

"We can stay competitive through education," replies Ronnie. "As the world advances, the countries with the best-educated citizens will do best."

A set of fair rules supposedly govern trade. New cars, the latest fashions, and electronic gizmos flow freely around the globe. Supply and demand control this. But tariffs are in place to protect developed nations' industries deemed critical or native.

Collecting a tariff, a tax, on rice from abroad keeps a major rice producing nation from losing home market share. And losing the jobs that go with it. The prosperous nations have specialized. Tariffs protect their specialties. The superpower's specialty now is weaponry for killing. A few other nations, including the other side, make nice warplanes and bombs. Supply and demand apply to war. But tariffs do not.

"What about workers and their children in distressed areas and in places where most people are still subsistence farmers?" says Ibrahim. "If we leave them behind, we create the conditions for social unrest, illegal trafficking, and war. People must eat. Parents will do what they must to feed their kids."

"We can't help everyone just because we're doing well," replies Ronnie. "Parents need to pull themselves up and assure the future by educating their children. Governments shouldn't meddle in education. Parents should control and pay for their own children's schooling. We shouldn't use taxes for education, even if others do," says Ronald.

Poor countries where most people still scrape a living from the land and where there are no abundant natural resources, have no tariffs. Natural resources and weapons flow into these nations at prices the market can bear. Almost no native products flow out. Princes of power still rule in these backwaters of the globe. And freedom is an illusion at best.

"Control of education prevents these things from changing," says Ibrahim. "Only the children of the wealthy have any chance of going to school in many places. These countries breed the cheap labor that makes parts for rich corporations. They provide the workers removed to other lands to sew the world's garments in sweatshops."

Ibrahim's brother and sister-in-law have prepared for this reality. They save for their own retirements. They do not count on anything from their employer or the government. They relied on government financing for their own educations. But they have paid off those debts. And they will not need more education loans. They intend to forgo the children they can't afford to raise and educate properly. They can remain in their 'starter' home. They'll have no need for more bedrooms or space for kids to play. And they won't support the economy by spending all of that money.

Ibrahim's brother and sister-in-law live well. They have a fairly new car, one of the world's best makes. They do not have to work in sweatshops. And they have that ten percent discount on all their electronics needs.

If only neither of them gets sick or injured as they age; they can continue to be proud to live in the only superpower in the universe.

There are two ways to improve the superpower's economy. The old-fashioned way is to create new or improved goods that other nations' citizens clamor to buy. Or to make familiar items at reduced prices. These things boost market share, creating good manufacturing jobs at home.

It was this system that fueled the superpower after the big World War. But the superpower has long since converted to a 'service economy'. It now produces little of actual value. Most of the nation's employees now do things like processing credit card receipts from those more robust nations.

The second way to bring in outside money is to raise tariffs. To make those nations that want to sell their goods in the superpower's large market pay a bribe. Consumers, of course, pay for tariffs in the end. Businesses adds them to the prices of goods and services.

Tariffs can go both ways. The superpower still does some things well besides death. Blessed with large plains that have a nearly perfect climate, it grows a good share of some of the world's foods. Well-to-do nations, seeing their sales limited by the superpower's tariffs, can retaliate with increased tariffs on the superpower's food.

Tariff wars have done a lot of economic damage in the past. With a service economy behind it and facing savvy competitor nations, the Ruling Class must try something else. They must do something brand new or something very old. They need to raise the people's perceived economic condition. Or they need to make them forget about it. The men in power believe they should use their new defensive weapon – a weapon of infinite coercion after all – to bend the world their way.

ALL WE ARE GIVEN

BOOK 5

Tolerance and In-Toleration

ALL WE ARE GIVEN

12 ALL IN THE FAMILY

Neil Valentine and Ibrahim Starks work closely together to integrate the ground and space based parts of SDS. Each man learns to trust and appreciate the other's fine qualities. They are both technically competent. And they work hard to master their new positions. Positions that others created just for the superpower's new weapon system.

They dedicate themselves to knowing and controlling every aspect of SDS that they can. They quickly define and staff their new organizations. To ensure continuity, they begin training their own replacements. Neil and Ibrahim are company men. And their competing companies, now providing SDS Support and Logistics Services together as a Joint Venture, are pleased to see it.

There is no break after tweaking each end of the system is finished. Or before the fine tuning of the whole system to work in syncopated rhythm begins. Ibrahim and Neil call their ends "heaven and hell." Ibrahim's problem with weak birds in space has no parallel on the ground. If a component fails tests on the ground, in Neil's 'hell', it gets replaced. There has been no failure deemed great enough to swap out an entire spacecraft over a faulty part.

Neil understands the difficulties in 'heaven' though. The two new coworkers and then friends get it as right as possible with the software patches and hardware available to them. The Final Exam is almost here.

A major religious holiday for most of the superpower's citizens arrives first. The Master Schedule recognizes this event. At nearly the same time, the real world test of SDS becomes possible. The Project Office postpones the test until after the break. Nearly everyone in Space Command and with the contractors will get to take some well deserved rest. Before finding out if tens of years of labor and their country's near economic ruin have succeeded in making a dream real.

Ibrahim is a confirmed bachelor who never had time for a wife or children. Neil is a family man. Neil Valentine invites Ibrahim Starks to join his family for the Holiday. Ibrahim accepts. It doesn't matter to either that the god whose Holiday they are to celebrate is Neil's but not Ibrahim's God. They are both in it for the good times: great food, a break from routines and deadlines, and companionship. That includes the warmth that Neil knows only a family can create.

Neil hopes that seeing the warmth and love in his family will make his new friend reconsider the benefits and rewarding duties of having a family. Neil is proud of his professional standing. But he is conscious every day that his family is his real reason for being.

After the meeting in the conference room, Mariam returned to the Control Room to watch over the telemetry from the probe. Graphing the data against projections shows how well the rocket performed. They have inserted the big ship and its as yet unused upper stage into orbit nicely. The Launch Director sees that the mission has begun well. The ship is almost precisely where it should be. And all onboard systems check out "right on the button."

Everyone in Mission Control congratulates Dr. Mariam and Sam Chakroborty. Their leaders then thank the assembled cast that did the deed. Mariam thanks all of the people beyond the walls of Mission Control and beyond the Launch Facility who lent their talents to the mission so far. From all the good will and harmony expressed, it's hard to imagine that anything other than a perfect launch occurred. The trouble at the North gate is still under investigation. But it seems forgotten now.

Mariam reviews the data from just before through just after the launch. She looks for anything unusual. The Launch Director makes damn sure the trouble did not compromise the launch in any way. Finally, Dr. Baker reads the notes and callbacks left for her during the conference room inquisition. Many of these are just congratulations. Her Assistant will reply with the usual "Thank you, and I couldn't have done it without 'so and so'." Some callbacks request technical information. Mariam farms these out to her Systems Control managers who are still at their consoles.

Mariam decides she has done all she can for the day in Mission Control. It's time to let her people do their work while she responds to her Assistant's note. The note she put aside earlier. Mariam wants desperately to talk to Representative Daegan. She is glad to hear that her friend, Jenny, is just down the hall in the Launch Director's offices.

Jenny made herself at home in Mariam's outer office. She commandeered a desk with a computer in a comfortable corner. She transferred her opening remarks for the NSEA Budget Review onto the machine.

"This is so much more efficient than using paper and regular mail or courier," Jenny thought. She sent her completed speech by email to both her office at home and the one in the Representatives Chambers building.

Mariam's Assistant brought Jenny a nice lunch from the cafeteria. She showed her to the office supplies. And she explained how to send email through the security locks that Space Launch Complex One uses.

"I'll have to tell Mariam how efficient her Assistant is," Jenny was thinking just as Dr. Baker walked into the room.

"You'd think I initiated a new World War by launching that space probe," says the Launch Director. She steps up to Representative Daegan and puts out her hand. Then she changes her mind and embraces her friend and confidant instead. "I've been wanting to ask what you thought of the fun today," Mariam says. The Director looks tired, preoccupied, and possibly a bit discouraged as well.

"I guess she's got a right," thinks Jenny. She did see Mariam corralled by Security men. But then guards removed Jenny from the Control Room. "What happened?" Jenny asks. "Did all those 'higher up' men grill you for doing your job in a cool fashion while they were running around losing control?"

Mariam and Jenny spent the next hour reliving less than ten minutes in time. Jenny tells Mariam what she observed in the Control Room. This includes the Executive Director huddling with two men before commanding Security to go after Mariam. It includes VIPs and NSEA personnel, some that likely had duties elsewhere, mobbing a station. The one with the speaker broadcasting the North gate news. And finally, there was the rush of Security personnel from outside the room to remove – well, Jenny for one.

Mariam recounted her thoughts just before pressing the big red button that committed the mission to launch. She knows she can trust Jenny never to tell anyone what those thoughts were. Jenny is the only person Mariam will ever entrust them with.

They go over Jenny's Opening Remarks for the NSEA Budget Review. Mariam makes some suggestions that add technical information. And they discuss in detail what Mariam fears will be lost if NSEA's budget is slashed. Jenny finally calls for her limousine and leaves the Launch Director alone in her offices.

On the return flight to Capitol Airport, Jenny's resolve to fight for the Agency and the NPCO programs stiffens even further as she mulls over what her friend said.

13 UNDER GOD

On the far side of the planet old time religion threatens to tear this globe apart. As the intelligence to nurture civilization and not just forge military alliances evolved, so did the need to understand the world. Superstition had explained things imagined and dreamed. Putting creation stories and oral histories on clay and then on paper froze organized religion. Measuring and recording the world and the cosmos created science.

Superstition explained the unknowable world in primitive times. Organized religion combined known history with the day's superstitions. Science learned to submit everything known and imagined to examination. And then to reexamination in light of the latest physical measurements.

People have now largely abandoned superstition. Science redefines itself with each new thing learned. It is an ongoing process of discovery and refinement. But organized religions remain fixed. They are immutable because gods wrote their tenets for all time. The gods are the problem. There are too many of them. Even too many of 'the One'. People are so committed to their personal gods, in search of something to believe in; that they are willing to kill each other for those beliefs. They do so in the name of God.

And there is a place on this planet where rabid religions and political affiliations stretching around the globe and down through time come to a nexus of nastiness. It is a small part of the planet. But it threatens an apocalypse for all.

In this place, one of the first where culture and civilization took root, three monotheistic religions vie for control. Crusading armies have thundered across this land in the name of God for much of recorded time. And they are thundering still today. Great teachers arose here. They taught peace and compassion for all. People recorded their messages as 'the word of God'. Then they perverted those words to cries of 'holy war'. Ancient prejudices and superstitions are nowhere near conquered here.

Now a surge in hatred threatens the globe from this place again. People have gone out; in the name of their one God and in reprisal for injustices imposed on them from afar; and they have committed acts of terrorism on civilians. They did this to people who are far, far removed in geography and understanding from this place. In response, those people sent an army. To create and ensure Security and freedom and access to resources.

With each round of these holy calamities, death and destruction have increased. The weapons that all of the one gods' armies possess now are frightening. Some of them are cunning and vile. The smallest incident rattles alliances world wide. The planet stands at a cliff's edge. People who are calling for religious intolerance, revival, or laws based on religion are calling for a war on peace. A war on all progress fraternal and technological. These religious fanatics and born-again moralists are baiting the very end of the world.

There are people from all sides of the conflict; religious and ethnic distinctions evident or not in the cut of their clothes, or in the color of their skin; who just want to move along with their businesses. Who want to ensure their means of providing for their families. They want to raise their children to be better than they perceive themselves to be. Often these souls are friends and even sometimes business partners with people who work in the next shop or stall. People whose god is not necessarily their God.

Many are willing to live side by side with people different from themselves. But their religious leaders and, seemingly, their holy texts say that only the righteous can ascend to heaven. And only they are righteous. All others must go to hell for their refusal to see.

Holy governments have expelled and repatriated ethnic and religious groups from this land again and again. Every god has some claim to every locale. Control of converted and reconverted shrines is reason enough to shed the blood of some parents' innocent child on any religious holiday. No one can propose a compromise that does not deny some one and only God its absolute supremacy. And they all raise again the cry to destroy or expel those who propose the compromise. Something brand new or something very old must be done.

14 HOME ALONE

Mariam Baker is at home. She sits idly watching television. The telephone sits nearby, but it has refused to ring so far today. After the dust settled at Space Launch Complex One, management held a formal Review. They examined the decision to launch the mission to the sister planet during the terrorist attack. This was quite different from the questioning Mariam underwent in the conference room. They generated tapes and transcripts and reports to prepare for the Review. They summarized and cross referenced these. They employed impressive visual aids that explained what the hell went on that day and what the hell was known about it. They invited people from afar. And they served refreshments at an appropriate break.

The NSEA-blue van that crashed the North gate was full of explosives. What the attackers intended those for is not known. Security people shooting at the van might have triggered the explosion. A defective triggering device might have caused it. Or it might have been set off on purpose by the people inside the blue van.

The van's incursion was the only thing found amiss that day at the Launch Complex. Except for two employees who took Personal Time off when they didn't have any accrued. They were suitably disciplined.

They found almost no remains of the attackers in the blue van. Nothing about their origins or identities could be determined.

DNA analysis detected only "four probably distinct sets of remains."

Raven's mother, Nancy, drove her to Gregory Kinkade's party. So that Raven could "— have fun without worrying about an automobile to park and then drive home afterwards." Mom, as usual, was worried and scared about her baby having grown up and gone out into the world to do adult things. Raven humored her as she long has. She appreciates dearly all of the things her mother does for her. There is an amazing ease and feeling of safety in being the child of a full time parent – in being "watched over." This is part of what gives Raven the courage to do the improbable in life.

Raven believes that someday she will want the family her dad talks about. She hopes she will be able to give her own children in turn what she has received. Raven intends to contribute to the world in works. It never occurs to her that what Nancy has given her children in love and direction is in any way of lesser value.

"Would you really leave the country or go to jail?" asks Micah.

"I don't know," Raven replies. "I did say it, didn't I? It came from somewhere inside of me, naturally." Micah, who has been concentrating on his driving while Raven called her mother, begins to relax. He's glad the weather is good and traffic is light.

"Raven, I'm scared for you," he blurts out. "This war shows signs only of getting bigger and going on without end. Doing the radical things you've talked about can hurt you in many ways. Not doing them, without an Exemption, can get you killed."

"Dear Micah, you care about me, don't you?" They haven't acknowledged this mutual feeling. It has been going on a long time. Micah's words make saying something about it easier for Raven. Micah admits his feelings too.

"Yes, Raven, I — just hoped you could tell. I care about you a lot."

When they pull up in the circular drive of the Winthrop mansion, before Raven walks to the door, she and Micah share a first kiss. Both are glad it happens.

"You are kind of a nerd though," Raven thinks as she walks through the big front entry and closes the door behind her.

Gregory's younger brother and sister helped him clean up the worst of the party. There wasn't that much to do. Greggy had expected several more hours of drinking. The sloppiness would have increased vastly in that time. There were a few drinks spilled on carpets. These weren't hard to clean. And there was nothing broken.

Gregory debated calling his parents to tell them about the Enforcement raid. Or leaving it alone until they hear from his uncle about the young Kinkades' fates.

When they finish cleaning, it looks like the house has seen a mild evening's fun. There is no evidence that anything ended badly or other than as expected. Gregory decides that the Kinkade offspring should just go off to bed.

The mission to the far side of the sun is on schedule, on trajectory, and possibly even on budget. Management ruled that Dr. Baker's decision to launch during the North Gate Incident was a temporary lapse of judgment. They removed Mariam from launch duty. She is to return to work two weeks before they lose communication with the probe. That will be when it passes behind the sun. They are paying Dr. Baker during her forced vacation. Which is now fast approaching its end.

Sam Chakroborty calls every day to keep Mariam up to speed on their mission. So far everything has gone as planned. The health of the spacecraft is excellent. The upper stage engine fired to propel the probe out of orbit. A slingshot maneuver around the big moon increased the bird's velocity in the direction opposite the planet's travel around the sun.

They have made two good course corrections. The craft is traveling away from home at nearly double the angular velocity at which the planet orbits the sun. The target is traveling about the same near circular course but in the opposite direction of the probe. The sister planet is traveling at exactly the home world's angular speed. And in the same direction. They calculate the time for the probe to intercept the sister planet at a little over three months, give or take.

It has been two and a half months since they launched the amazing probe. Mariam's Leave began two months ago. There should have been one other space shot from Launch Complex One during this time. They postponed it for 'administrative' reasons.

"This last week before I return will be the hardest," Mariam thinks. Every week has been the hardest for the Launch Director whose life is her work. Having no children of her own, Dr. Baker watches over each mission she helps command with the same loving attention people give their progeny. If hardware had hope, Dr. Mariam's spacecraft would be inspired to do the improbable time and time again.

"The instruments on the probe will be unpacked beginning the day after I return," Mariam recalls. There are booms to extend, to distance some instruments from the body of the spacecraft. Or to distance them from other sensors. The electricity generating 'wings' must be released. And they will unfurl the big, high gain antenna.

"Deploying large components is always tense," she reflects. "There are calibrations that need to be performed. We need to make sure the instruments are working properly before encountering the target. We believe the craft itself; propulsion, communications, computer, and electrical storage; is healthy," Mariam thinks. "But we have no idea yet if its instruments can record anything when it gets there."

Sam calls Mariam at last. Nothing has changed in the last twenty-four hours. And they haven't attempted anything new.

"We're just monitoring the telemetry. We're waiting for the last ground controlled course correction opportunity day after tomorrow," Sam says. "I doubt we'll fire up the engine. The course looks virtually perfect already. I'm guessing we'll hoard fuel even if there is some small discrepancy, so the ship has it to use later."

"The truth," says Mariam, "is that the unknowns can now be bigger than any course changes we'd make. We could be 'correcting' in the wrong direction, given the uncertainties. We've proven the engines and their control systems with the first two burns. It's better to save wear and tear in case those systems get a real workout later."

ALL WE ARE GIVEN

BOOK 6

High Ground and Revelation

ALL WE ARE GIVEN

15 BROTHERS

Following morning worship, the brothers Akheron linger in the Temple. They listen to the visiting Cleric's call for action against the invaders from far, far away. They have heard this call from many Prayer Leaders and scholars over the years. But their father always guides them from answering with their souls. They, or at least the youngest of the three, are too young to make such decisions – such supreme commitments.

Akheron, their father, is a merchant who sells cloth and robes in his own shop. Father is very successful. They have three sisters back home with their mother in their large, traditional home. They must hurry to father's shop now, as the Holy Days are fast approaching. There are many customers buying. Father needs their help in his shop.

The brothers linger a little longer to hear the Revered scholar read from the Holy Book. The words from the Book speak of the One God and His desire that His children should be strong and worship Him properly. And thus arise into Heaven. Only children who follow their God's commands will receive a great reward in the hereafter. Only the One God is God. He alone is to be worshiped. All others are false. All of those assembled have heard these words read many times before.

The Revered Cleric and great scholar tells the gathered men that the strength the Book speaks of is willingness to sacrifice self. To achieve God's purpose here, now, and forever after. There will be no heaven for people who worship other gods. Nor for those who worship the One God but not in the manner called for in the Book. There will be no reward for those who live in other than the Book's Holy ways. Such people are sores and cankers on the society of true believers. Believers must cast them out and remove their influence from the city, the nation, and the world.

The Cleric calls for all who are able, to come to a special school. There they will learn to battle the invaders, their false gods, and their unholy ideas wherever they are found.

Baruch, the oldest, rushes his younger brothers toward the market after they leave the Temple. They are late. Their father will not be pleased. He worshiped earlier and left before his sons. Father will know that they have been listening to the traveling Cleric. When they should have been working for the family's continued success.

As the brothers pass through the streets in the early morning, they see many soldiers and vehicles of the occupying army. They pass knots of local men who cast glances at the soldiers. These men talk in whispers. They do not want anyone beyond their own group to hear them.

Baruch keeps a wary eye on everything as he herds his brothers quickly along. He loves his brothers as life itself. Being the oldest, his father has charged him with watching over them. Some of the soldiers seem interested in the boys. They call after them. The brothers know that the soldiers have strange and delicious foreign candy to offer. However, they know that where there are soldiers there may be fighting. And death for anyone too close.

Baruch keeps away from crowds of his own people too. He tries to stay where they can run easily if trouble happens. He has seen sudden clashes between patriots and the evil foreign soldiers leave many dead who were only in the wrong place.

With a roar to silence God himself and a huge flash of orange fire, a car on the other side of the narrow street leaps into the air. The explosion blows the three sons of Akheron into the wall of the house nearest them.

Baruch awakes slowly as from a dream. There is shouting all around. A pile of twisted metal sputters and pops as it burns in the street. Baruch vaguely sees people running here and there. He hears guns firing. There are people lying in the street. As his eyes clear, Baruch sees that some of those people do not move at all. One near him lies in a growing pool of red.

When he clears his mind and looks about farther, Baruch finds his youngest brother lying twisted and still. There is a bright smear of red on the wall where his thin form leans and a small pool of it beneath him. The youngest Akheron brother, Baruch's charge and one of the lights in his family's life, seems strangely peaceful. And he will stay that way in his oldest brother's memory until the end of Baruch's own time.

Wailing and stumbling often for the tears in their eyes and the pain in their limbs, the remaining sons of Akheron carry their fallen brother to their father's house. They take him to his mother. People arrive who want to clean and bandage the boys' wounds. But the sons of Akheron will not allow that yet. Their father arrives and the entire family grieves over the little body. Over this and the next days, relatives from all over the city come to grieve.

This house, like so many now in the occupied city, will never again be the happy place it was. Baruch proclaims to all that he must atone for the death. His father charged him with keeping his brothers safe. He failed in the task.

The mourning time is nearly done. The Holy Days have passed and their brother's young soul has gone to its reward. The remaining sons of Akheron approach their father again with an often repeated request. They would go to the Religion School outside a nearby city, the school the Cleric in the Temple told of. There they will prepare in piety to avenge their brother's death at the hands of the foreigners.

Their mother, hearing this plan and seeing her husband consider it, cries again for her littlest one and for all her sons. She knows there is almost sure death in this path. She cries as well for her daughters. Who must live in a time when brothers and fathers and husbands may all be killed. In the name of God, and of Security and freedom, and access to resources.

Their Revered father wishes more than anything to keep his sons with his family. He would watch over them as they grow and marry and have children of their own to protect and raise and teach life's mysteries. He wants to see his sons acquire wisdom in their roles as husbands and fathers. He knows that this wisdom can be obtained in no other way.

Akheron knows however, that the day must come when his sons stand on their own. When they can make life's decisions and go on as adults without him. Surely, he would come to the end of his own time before the death of another child.

Akheron gives his remaining sons permission to pursue their fates and their souls' wishes in the school a day's journey from their home. He bids them to consider the very words they read in the Holy Book. Not just what some claim the meanings are. He is a devout man himself and believes wholly in the Word of God. Akheron's wife and the boys' mother grieves once more as the brothers leave home. She knows she is unlikely to see them alive again.

16 ALL THEY CAN BE

Mariam fusses over this detail and she fusses over that one.

"How could they have kept me from my charges all this time?" Dr. Baker has been back at work for nearly a week. She has already presided over a launch from the same pad the probe to the other side of the sun flew from. It was a minor launch, previously postponed for some reason. It put a small satellite into low orbit to study the atmosphere's boundary. The launch came off without a hitch. But they are having trouble now with the satellite's communication system.

Mariam suspects that Launch Quality Control didn't do its job with the satellite's main antenna. It looks like the antenna isn't going to deploy. The fixed, low gain antenna will be the only means of relaying information. The satellite might still complete its primary objectives this way. But it will take additional budget for the lengthened time to download the data over a low bandwidth channel. There is some worry about the satellite's stabilizing and pointing systems having enough fuel for an extended mission. And drag from the thin, wispy edge of the atmosphere might slow the satellite enough to bring it crashing down to a fiery reentry death too soon.

Mariam has been working on the capstone to her career as well. Space Launch Command began sending instructions to the amazing probe soon after she returned to work. Now it is only days until the rendezvous with the sister planet. There is a lot of work to do. Every step is critical to the success of this mission. This is perhaps the greatest mission of exploration and discovery of all time. Mariam can hardly believe how elated, worried, and useful she feels as she shepherds the probe and the organization that launched it into the heavens. She carefully provides the probe with its final instructions as it nears its unknowable future.

The probe's instruments began waking up on commands from the ship's computer. The bird must warm some sensors to make them function properly. It turns on electric heaters to do that. Some devices need to be at temperatures near absolute zero. Even in space, this near the sun, objects are not that cold. The ship turns on an electronic refrigeration system. It plunges a gas far below oxygen's freezing point. The gas becomes a liquid. The computer opens valves and turns on a pump. That circulates the incredibly cold fluid through those sensors. Telemetry beams the status of all these operations back home.

It takes a lot of electrical power to perform these changes. And it will take more to perform even greater changes on commands from the ground.

They charged the spacecraft's batteries just before launch. The probe has a few small photovoltaic cells fixed on its exterior. These were operating at liftoff. But the ship hasn't enough power to change into the potent engine of investigation it needs to be when it meets its target. The bird needs to spread its wings to make the really big changes.

Two large photovoltaic arrays or 'wings' were folded compactly on the probe when it was launched. High strength covers have helped protect them from micrometeorites that might have destroyed them. Now it's time to unfold the wings. It is time to expose them to the sun to generate enough electrical power to make other changes. And for continuous operation of the ship' instruments.

Mariam recalls the debate that resulted in this design and mission profile.

"There are two systems able to provide enough electrical power to run a monster craft like this," she thinks. "A delicate photovoltaic system must be stowed to protect it during launch. The other system is a radioisotope thermoelectric generator or RTG. An RTG is a device that converts the heat of radioactive decay into electricity. It is small, rugged, and functional at liftoff. Photovoltaic wings are huge. They are not functional at liftoff.

"It might have seemed a simple choice except for the fear of anything nuclear by some people. RTGs have flown before," she thinks. "But only with fear in some of the populace that they might come tumbling down to break open and spread radioactivity everywhere. This fear is not entirely unfounded. A launch failure is always possible. But existing designs make the area of contamination at a launch quite small."

In the end a different but related argument gave the probe its wings.

"The possibility of life on the sister planet drove the choice," Mariam remembers. "Even though some argued that there can't be life elsewhere as God created it only here."

Wherever people have explored in our system, they have found only dry and airless moons, moons with toxic atmospheres, and extremely hot or cold planets. Scientists believe these are incapable of supporting complex life. No one has seen the mysterious sister planet except in faint, low resolution photos from deep space. But its similar size and distance from the sun might duplicate surface conditions on the home world.

"The fear that a nuclear-powered probe falling from deep space at extreme speed into a dense atmosphere could widely contaminate a populated world won out. The bird grew wings instead," recalls Mariam.

It's up to Mariam and the Mission Team headed by Sam to see that the wings deploy. The mission will fail without them. Their small folded sizes minimized the chance of micrometeorite hits. Now it's time to jettison the covers and unfold the wings. Without them the ship cannot generate the electricity it needs to proceed. Micrometeorites will hit and destroy some of the small, independent panels covering their surfaces during the mission. But the wings are oversized to allow for these losses.

Sam gives the order, with Mariam looking on, to blow the covers from the wings by igniting explosive bolts. It takes nearly forty minutes for the instructions to cross the vast distance and a reply to return. Telemetry tells Sam and Mariam that sensors have recorded the covers clearing the ship.

"We should get photos that show this later, after the big

antenna is deployed. And just before the ship disappears behind the sun," thinks Sam. Two onboard cameras are, hopefully, recording such events. And they're recording the view of the sister planet that is now visible from the spacecraft. High resolution photos take too much time to transmit on the currently available channel.

Electrical checks show that both wings' circuits are good. So, orders go out to turn the craft by firing very small rocket engines or thrusters. They align the wings' electric motors with the warming sun. The ship slowly unfolds its wings and extends their supporting booms. Four hours later the wings are out and locked in place. They are facing the sun. And the solar tracking system is holding that orientation. The wings are charging the ship's batteries.

Mariam decides she can go home for the night and recharge her own batteries. She asks Sam to call if anything unexpected happens. He and members of his team will take turns through the night sitting at a console to monitor electrical system and battery conditions. They will sleep on cots while off duty.

Jenny Daegan's phone call early the next day interrupts Mariam's morning routine.

"It's true, Mariam. The Economic Stabilization Program Office is going to reexamine the Agency's budget. They will consider all NPCO programs for cuts. Including those with missions scheduled and ones with spacecraft under contract for construction."

The President, as directed by the Prime Minister, has ordered that all NSEA missions not fully funded be frozen. Except for military space programs. ESP will review even funded nonmilitary programs. They will determine the 'close out' costs of terminating them – paying off the corporations' contracts. The Leadership is planning another round of Corporate Tax Reductions for Competitiveness. Along with new capital gains tax cuts.

The tax cuts on stock profits will be "— for companies and individuals contributing directly to the nation's economy. For those whose investments in the means of production provide gainful employment for the nation's populace. And for those who have suffered from taxation of their rightful estates."

The ESP Office must wrest the means to provide these large tax cuts from the budget. A 'fiscally conservative' party can defend funding by borrowing only for so long. They have already cut social programs that would ensure a brighter future. They cut funds for many improvements to education. Those are now jokes – 'mandates without money'.

Dr. Baker's nightmare is coming true.

"At least the mission to the planet on the far side of the sun is out there and safe from bureaucratic foolishness," Mariam thinks.

Micah spent weeks after his Finals searching for an eight to five job to fill time until the new school year begins. And to give him some real world experience. He finally found an Internship with one of the largest engineering firms on the globe. The firm just opened a slot in the capitol for a new graduate or a graduate student.

The Internship has the potential to become a permanent position. If both the firm and the Intern think it's a good fit. Micah doesn't intend to stay with the job beyond the break. He has one more year to finish his graduate program. He is not going to drop that now even for a lucrative, high profile post.

Micah is glad that his new job utilizes his technical skills, without requiring too much from him in the way of weighed decision making. This is Micah's first professional position. He has book smarts. But he knows that only experience can give him the wisdom to make good decisions involving resource, schedule, and technical trade-offs.

Gregory, new graduate and crown of his family, finds a good job close to home too. The firm whose offer he accepts is just across the border in the next state. Greggy leases a one bedroom apartment on the opposite side of the capitol's sprawling suburbs from his parents' place. He wants to be near the firm that seems very pleased to hire him. He can be back at his parents' home quickly for any evening or weekend Kinkade affair he chooses to attend. It's just an hour's drive.

The Kinkades are proud of their first ever Upper School graduate. Greggy outfits his first apartment with a new bed, a new couch, and a new top of the line sound system. He keeps his old furnishings in his room at his parents' house. Now he has two places he can call home.

Greggy's parents forgave him almost immediately for the Enforcement raid of the party. They heard the next day from Dad's brother that the Agents let the boys go shortly after taking them to the Enforcement Station. Greggy's cousins did not have drinks in hand when they were arrested. The Agents did not field test them for sobriety. And a few checks showed their 'suspicious car parked out of sight around the far corner' to be nothing more than their car. Of course, the Agents had the car towed for being suspicious. Greggy's cousins had to pay the towing and impound fees.

Not much else came from the aborted party. Except that they found a drunk named Dick to be underage by a week. Dick did have a drink in hand. Enforcement arranged for Dick to meet both his military Obligation date and his debt to society. Dick spent the first month of his enlistment in the military stockade.

17 GREETINGS

"Welcome, ladies and gentlemen. And welcome esteemed Representatives, Mr. Secretary, and my fellow Orators. I wish to open this Review of the National Space Exploration Agency's General Budget by drawing your attention to a most significant event. One that is taking place as we meet in this historic Chamber," began Representative Jeannette Daegan.

Jenny described the probe to the sister planet and its mission of discovery. She listed the breakthrough technologies that NSEA and contractor scientists and engineers created just to meet the probe's mission needs. She showed how these are already changing computer chips, manufacturing controls, and more.

Orator Daegan showed the nation and its corporations the large economic paybacks they are getting from their small investment in the NSEA probe.

"I ask you to consider this efficient and effective Agency's budget request as if it were no more than a financial investment," said Jenny. "Nowhere can you find a better return on your dollar. Or a more historically secure place to put these tax dollars. Than in the budgets of the National Space Exploration Agency and its Near Planets and Celestial Objects programs. Such as the probe passing behind these worlds' star now, as I speak."

"Let's configure this spacecraft for its rendezvous with history," says Launch Director Baker. She sweeps into the Mission Control Room. She disturbs Sam's sleeping colleagues.

It hasn't been an hour since she talked with Representative Daegan on the phone. Mariam has decided that what will be in the Capitol, will be. That is out of her hands and up to people like Jenny. What she, Mariam, can do is her job. And Dr. Baker is always happy to do her job.

"Sam, how're the batteries looking?"

"Fine, Mariam, just fine. The photovoltaic circuits and control systems are nominal. We've got full charges on all the batteries. We can go ahead and deploy the instrument booms and the high gain antenna. And we can test and calibrate the last sensors."

"Let's get started then. We've only got a few hours before the bird slips out of sight behind the sun. I argued with this last second timing. But the Principal Investigators for the mission were worried. They feared too much damage to the wings and the big antenna. They won.

"We need to make sure everything is as right as we can make it before we lose signal. We'll download the large files that the ship has recorded so far. I'm anxious to see the target as the robot sees it now. These will be the best pictures ever taken of our sister planet until the ones taken from orbit. The pictures we don't get to see until, and unless, our bird reemerges from behind the sun."

They command the big spacecraft to turn one way and then another over the next three and a half hours. This lets the sun warm each telescoping instrument boom as it extends. The sunning warms the actuation motors. The booms themselves don't need it. They chose graphite epoxy composite for the booms in part because of the way it behaves in the extreme temperatures of space. It hardly expands or contracts – possibly warping and binding – with temperature at all.

With the booms fully extended, the danger of any whipping motion caused by their deployment is over. They order the large high gain antenna to shed its protective sheath and fan out to its full diameter.

While these changes are going on, the ultra-cooled infrared camera is taking photos of 'warm' equipment on the ship. They test and calibrate other instruments. At the end of six hours of work, telemetry says that the robot is ready to perform as advertised. The probe transmits its first large files, including visible light photographs of the planet, just before the signal abruptly ends. It is replaced with space static. "Wow!" exclaims everyone as they stare at the high resolution photos displayed on the big monitors.

Raven and her mother, Nancy, are looking at yet another loft apartment. They have been hunting for what will become Raven's studio and living quarters for weeks now without success. The problem is the budget. It's slim.

"I will not help you endanger your life, daughter," Markus said with a weighty sigh. Raven had asked him to help her get started in life beyond academia. Markus did not cut Raven off entirely. But he hoped to make leaving home difficult enough to make her reconsider graduate school.

There would not be a loan to help Raven move out of the family home.

"The home that we now keep just for you, dear. Seeing as your older brother and sister no longer live with us," said Markus. Raven can take her car when she leaves. Markus and Nancy will continue to carry her on their health insurance. But she must acquire an auto policy of her own.

"Of course, all the furniture in your rooms is yours to dispose of or move to new quarters as you see fit," Markus said.

"I don't know if I can keep looking, Mom. This is the least expensive place we've seen and it barely has enough space for me. Also, I'm not crazy about the neighborhood." Raven glances from the fourth storey windows down onto a somewhat tough looking commercial street.

"It does have a security garage for your car though, dear," replies Nancy. "I think it would be just fine. And it's close to home in case you need anything or just want to visit your mother."

Raven had totaled up her life savings and estimated her costs for food, utilities, insurance, and art supplies. She divided the balance after three months' expenses to determine the budget for her new space. She believes she can begin making enough money to keep herself in that time. Raven is willing to gamble on the improbable.

"Take this apartment, Raven," says her mother. "I know the neighborhood. It's not far from where I grew up. You'll find that it's not that bad. I'll help you with the rent if you need me to for as long as my own money holds out. I want you to have the start you think you should have, daughter. Take this apartment." And Raven does.

Gregory arrives home from his new job on a Friday afternoon. He's planning on a free weekend and a pleasant drive to his other home to see the family. He idly locks his car, gathers his mail from the box out front, and steps inside his neat but still rather sterile pad. After Greggy gets a snack from the nearly empty refrigerator, he sorts the mail on his kitchen table.

"Here's something interesting," he thinks as he opens a letter from the Federal government. Inside he reads the one-word salutation, 'Greetings'. Then he notices the letterhead of the Joint Military Services. Gregory has been invited to a war. And attendance is mandatory.

18 HOME FOR THE HOLIDAYS

Neil Valentine's family has been cleaning and decorating their home for a week to prepare for the Holidays. Neil's wife is a stay at home parent for good reason. A full time parent is needed to watch over such a large family. The Valentine's are eight happy souls: Valencia, Neil, and their six children – three boys and three girls.

Their oldest child, a girl, is nearing graduation from public school and looking into higher education. Their youngest, also a girl, is five years old and "just really getting interesting," according to her father. Neil has considered each of his children fascinating from their very first breaths of this world's air. He was present for all of those first breaths. He has been a devoted father to each of his children since then. And Neil will continue to be so until the end of his own time.

"Of course, invite your friend to come for the Holidays," Valencia said when Neil proposed Ibrahim as a houseguest. The Valentine house is modest in appearance. But it is quite large and includes a guest bedroom with a private bath, more or less. Both sets of grandparents visit often. But they are all busy elsewhere this Holiday season. The rooms kept presentable for them are available.

"What are we going to do with this Ibrahim?" asked Valencia.

"Just let him enjoy a holiday with a happy family, my dear," replied Neil. "He's a bachelor, although a very nice guy whom I'm guessing will be fine with the kids. I think he could be more than a bachelor with the right incentive, if you know what I mean."

"Then, should I be thinking of providing that incentive? Tell me how old he is and what he's like and I might invite over some appropriate female friends of mine. Give me enough reason to believe the 'nice guy' part, and I might even invite a relative of the right gender."

Ibrahim often stays with his brother and sister-in-law on the holidays they celebrate. They invite him for all of God's major festivals. He is glad to get away when he can take time off work. He flies to the city where his relatives live. He goes to worship among friends and fellow believers. And to play with his brother's newest electronic toys.

Ibrahim doesn't celebrate this coming holiday, although he gets the time off work. It is the major festival of the majority of the populace's god. He doesn't have to fly anywhere to accept the Valentines' invitation. Neil and his family live nearby. And as he understands it, there won't be any real worshiping. There will be no awkward times when he can't participate. It seems more like a big birthday celebration. Everyone will receive favors, enjoy good food, and probably get to play with the latest games.

Ibrahim is not sure how he will get along with the Valentine children. He remembers being a child, of course. He recalls fondly, if faintly, being with his own siblings and young friends. When he lived in the land of his parents and grandparents. Ibrahim doesn't interact with children now. His brother and sister-in-law don't have any. It has been a long time since he knew anyone who did. Being with the Valentine children doesn't worry him. But Ibrahim was thinking about it as he arrived at the Valentines' home.

Ibrahim brought a gift of food for Neil's family. He found out that wine or liquor are common gifts for this festival. But his own religion strictly forbids drugs. Ibrahim follows God's teachings in this regard. He knows that much food will be provided. Ibrahim brought the Valentines a dessert. One he chose to compliment whatever else was served. He brought them a fruitcake.

Ibrahim is not strict and he doesn't expect anyone else to comply with his standards. But he still practices his own religion's basic tenets. He will not provide a drug to his friend's family. But Ibrahim will sit at the table where it is served. Living in a land full of people who have other ways and who worship other gods has taught him some tolerance.

"Be sure to lock the doors so you're not interrupted by the younger children," Valencia told Ibrahim as she and Neil showed him his rooms. "Especially the bathroom doors." That afternoon Ibrahim moved his car to the driveway to get it off the narrow street. He unpacked and hung his clothes in the guest room closet. And he enjoyed a shower in his semi-private bathroom. Then Ibrahim sat down to the first family dinner with young children at the table that he could recall ever.

Ibrahim enjoys the children's laughter and their curiosity toward him. He is intrigued by the other guest for dinner that evening, one of Valencia's female friends. Who just happens to be about his age and unmarried. Ibrahim avoids being too familiar with Neil's wife. As his parents taught him. But he finds this young woman who sits next to him at dinner a joy to talk to. And hard not to make eye contact with.

Most of the Valentines' holiday decorations are unlike those used in his God's festivities. But Ibrahim likes that the Valentines dress their home for the celebration. The scented candles remind Ibrahim of his childhood. The holiday music playing over and over, with Mrs. Valentine and various children sometimes singing along, feels like home too. And the sense of tradition with which the family speaks of their favorite decorations reminds Ibrahim of nearly forgotten memories. Memories from his own time as a child, watched over by his own loving parents.

On his third evening with the Valentines, in the middle of learning a new electronic game, Ibrahim has a realization. He is jealous of the children's closeness to their parents. As an adult, he converts that jealousy to a desire. The desire to assume the rewarding responsibilities of being the watcher rather than the watched.

The actual celebration of this god's birthday comes on a cold morning. All of the family and Ibrahim awake very early. They turn on the holiday lights and music, light the scented candles, and begin unwrapping the presents. Ibrahim had watched the presents accumulate for days, as relatives visited leaving gifts for all. And picking up gifts from the Valentines for aunts, uncles, nieces, nephews, and cousins.

Ibrahim smiles seeing that the bulk of the gifts are for the little ones. He sees Neil and Valencia exchange gifts. There are presents to and from Ibrahim as well. After the presents and a special morning meal, Ibrahim and Neil sit talking while overlooking the remains of the unwrapping. The topic turns to work and the coming test of SDS.

"I hope with all my heart that the system is never needed," says Neil. "I have helped construct it only because I believe it is a necessary evil."

"I don't expect it ever will be used," replies Ibrahim. "It is the best hope to end the threat of attack with Intercontinental Missiles by anyone on anyone. I believe that was the intent of the people who dreamt it and specified it. The cost has been almost beyond calculation. But if it prevents the end of the world it will have been worth it. I realize that when I have children and grandchildren of my own, they too will have to help pay for the thing. I pray they will live in peace and security because of it."

"I hope you are right, my friend, says Neil."

"Thanks for coming, Ibrahim! We've enjoyed having you here. You made our Holidays brighter by being with us this year,"

Neil and Valencia tell him as he pulls out of their driveway. Ibrahim turns his car toward his empty home.

Ibrahim is sorry to see his time with the Valentines end. With a New Year about to begin and a major task to face immediately at work, there is hardly time to ponder the old year. Or to wonder at the changes wrought in these days spent with Neil's family. Ibrahim knows he is changed. He looks at the world in a different way now. And he finds himself thinking again and again of the little slip of paper he brings home from his holiday. The one with a young woman's phone number on it.

Three religions and two holidays commingle and collide on the other side of the world. New religions borrow traditions from earlier ones. This helps people transition to the latest gods. The early gods were plentiful. They were often based on observations from nature such as the domains or 'elements' of fire, water, air, and earth; the seasons of the planet; or the repetitive events seen in the heavens. The cataloging of physical traits and natural events ultimately created science and rational thought. But rational thought is not what is happening in this small part of the planet now.

The coincidence of festivals of the One Gods was inevitable. All new religions use dates from early 'pagan' rites. It could be worse. All three of these One Gods' celebrations could be demanding center stage at once.

The brothers Akheron had been in the Religion School a few weeks when the Revered Teachers sent the younger brother back to his father's house. He is small and too young to make the supreme commitment they have already received from Baruch. The scholars are wise men but they are practical too. Akheron needs a son to help with and to learn the business. The household is a devout and traditional one. It reflects well on God's plan. Such a house deserves a son to carry on the name of Akheron. The younger boy is the Clerics' gift to that house.

Baruch is filled with the Holy spirit. He is eager to bring death to the usurpers – the occupiers of God's land and murderers of his youngest brother. The Revered Teachers judge him sufficient contribution to the cause.

A young male again blesses the Akheron household with his presence. His mother has a boy to spoil at home. His Revered father has a son to teach the business. And to accompany him to worship in the Temple.

"It's good to see one of your sons helping in your shop again, my friend," says the man who owns the business next door. It is early morning. Akheron and his son have just arrived from worship to open their shop.

"Once more I must express my deep sorrow at the loss of your youngest one."

The man in the next shop does not sell robes but he does sell cloth. He sells cloth intended for uses other than in robes – heavy cloth for wall hangings and furniture coverings. He and Akheron have worked together on occasion to fill large, lucrative orders of finished goods for the finest houses in the city. With Akheron's machines to finish the articles and his neighbor's selection of cloth suitable for the purpose, they make a fine joint venture. The man in the adjacent shop does not worship the same god that Akheron does.

"I miss the littlest one more than anyone other than God can know," replies Akheron. "My oldest son is in Religion School studying in all piety. This one is my salvation in this world, my center of the universe for now. I find the most joy when he accompanies me to daily worship in the Temple."

"My God's celebration is approaching fast," his friend tells Akheron. "I have need for joining and hemming cloth to complete my customers' orders for the rituals. Will you help me again to fill these needs? Will our arrangements for payment be the same?"

"I can help you of course, my friend," replies Akheron. "The business is good for both of our houses. Will you be worshipping more as this festival approaches? I do not understand when you go to your temple. You do not close as I do during the day for worship."

"Our religion calls us to worship together once a week. I will close for the celebration day though. It comes not on our Sabbath this year but on another day of the week. I must have all my orders filled before then."

"I am surprised that you worship so seldom. Is this in accord with your holy book?" Akheron knows that this other side has a holy book too. But not the Holy Book that contains the real Word of God.

"We are called to keep the Sabbath Holy. We do that by worshipping together and not conducting business on that day. We also pray in our own homes many times each week."

"It is different than my Holy Book requires," thinks Akheron. "But it is his way and I can tell he is a pious man."

Another celebration will begin soon. It is the eight day festival of the third religion struggling for control in this small part of the globe. Akheron does not understand this holiday's timing at all. It varies so each year. But he loathes its coming. His neighbor in the next shop wants only to live in the land where so many of his religion's shrines and monuments are. These others wish to make the land their own. They want to control the Holy places and Holy cities and marginalize or even cast out God's own people. Akheron has no use for followers of a religion that would steal the very land of his ancestors.

In truth, the precedence of claims on the land is lost in the mists of time. These three religions have existed in this small place, on and off, for millennia.

Akheron harbors loathing too for those of his friend's faith who live far, far away from this Holy land. These outsiders support those who would rob Akheron's people of their heritage. The outsiders themselves came long ago in great numbers to 'reclaim' the land for their religion. They waged holy wars against the very will of the One True God. They were beaten back time and time again. There are those of Akheron's faith who say the army now from far, far away is another such crusade.

"You have no work for the cursed ones, I assume. I will not help to sew a single robe for them or for one of their divans," says Akheron.

"No, I do not ask that of you," says his neighbor.

"Then we have no problem. If you took orders for them requiring my machines, I could not in faith be involved."

Baruch's religious instruction at the school continues night and day. It seems he is always in class or at worship. Many of the students are older than Baruch. They are often the eldest sons of their families. Baruch studies hard. He truly wishes to be like his Revered father: a devout man.

After a while there are things for Baruch to do other than reading and discussing the Holy texts and showing his devotion to God through prayer. Baruch receives instructions for making weapons with which to take revenge on the usurpers.

Baruch recalls his father's words. He knows that the patriarch of his family would say the Holy Book contains nothing good about the taking of life. Still, the Revered Teachers are the ones providing the instructions. They must know the true path to spiritual fulfillment and establishment of God's righteous plan. Soon his teachers will provide Baruch with more than just printed instructions for making Holy War.

BOOK 7

Art of War

ALL WE ARE GIVEN

ALL WE ARE GIVEN

19 WAR PRAYERS

The planet's New Years celebrations are over. It's a curious thing, this 'new year'. Most of the planet has agreed on a secular calendar based on knowledge of the planet's rotation around its star. But some religions still maintain their own calendars based on accepted superstition. These calendars still use eight month years, twelve month years, thirteen month years, and more. The definitions of a month are numerous. Some systems question the whole concept of a month. People still use calendars that ignore the planet's seasons and the cyclic phenomena visible in the sky.

Multiple calendars confuse people like Akheron. People who are just trying to understand the timing of various gods' festivals. They make as much sense as some forgotten king's foot and twelfths of that being the length standard of a land. When a simpler and nearly universal system exists. Confusion over measurement systems is likely to cost someone an expensive spacecraft or two someday.

Ibrahim and Neil present their evidence to Space Command and to the big brass on both sides of the Joint Venture. The defensive system, SDS, is ready to try to shoot something down. The brasses take it 'under advisement'. A lot of people who know less than the Contractor specialists will review the data and analysis. They'll look for mathematical and logical errors. And try to find judgment calls they can dispute. Finally, the government technical specialists pass the word down to Neil and Ibrahim and up to Space Command. The test is a 'go'.

"Thanks again, my friend, for the great time I had at your family's home over the holiday," says Ibrahim.

"We were glad to have you there," replies Neil. "Did you find our children a problem?"

"No, not at all. In fact, I understand what you hold so precious now, Neil. I believe I will have some children of my own some day."

"Not without a partner you won't, Ibrahim. And did you find my wife's friend an interesting woman, eh?"

"Yes." says Ibrahim. "But I cannot speak of such things. Now, about the schedule for the test. The launch from the atoll, four thousand eight hundred kilometres out in the ocean, will happen day after tomorrow. That's the schedule, anyway. I understand that Space Command has had people working on that for weeks, right through the holiday. Do you agree that we can be ready by then?"

"I believe we are ready now," says Neil. "As you know, even though this is supposed to be a 'complete test', certain parts of the system will be in 'test mode'. This will prevent things like mobilization of forces outside of SDS Command; automated Federal bulletins on the public airwaves; and the panic that might result from a complete real world test. Space Command has been flipping switches and pushing buttons already this morning to enter test mode. I believe they have finished. We are just waiting for a target to present itself."

Greggy arrived at his parents' home early Friday evening. Everyone there was happy to see him, including his two cousins and their parents. They had come for dinner. These are the cousins now widely known to drive a suspicious vehicle.

Everyone had a good laugh reliving the Enforcement raid in detail over the meal. Greggy's sister and brother told their stories too. They stood on the landing half-way up the stair to the second storey. They watched the interrogations in the living room below them. They followed the Agents who checked the upper floor. The adults were surprised to learn that looking for minors drinking required close examination of closet and bookshelf contents.

Gregory's uncle's family leaves. His own family settles in for the night. Then Greggy shows his parents the letter from the

Federal government.

"Perhaps something can be done about it," says his father. "Can your job get you an Exemption?"

"There must be something to do about it!" fumes his mother. "Our only Upper School graduate and the pride of this family is not going off to die in the Leadership's dirty little war on the other side of the planet!"

"I will double check, of course, when I get back to work on Monday. But they told me when I hired on that the position is not Essential to the war effort.

"I can try to find a new job – fast – that does qualify. Or I can accept that I have been Chosen. Then I will go off to wherever they decide, to do whatever they say. I can only hope my great job will still be here for me as promised by law. If I ever return. Or I can do something else. Our neighbors to the north can use my technical skills. I am thinking of leaving the country."

This brings the whole Kinkade family to attention. Greggy's brother and sister have heard him tell his parents before that he might consider this to avoid going to war. That he does not generally believe in war. He has no faith in this war's justifications. And that he will not be forced to kill his fellow beings. For Security or for access to resources or to make 'right' their religious preferences.

"Greggy, if you go you can never come back," moans his sister. "I have a friend at school whose brother moved to avoid forcedsac. His parents say they will never speak to him again."

"Well, that wouldn't happen in this family," their father says.

"You won't have any family or friends in a new country," adds his brother. "You'll lose so much. We were talking about this in school the other day. Our teacher said that even if traitors are allowed to come back someday, they'll be shunned by all true patriots."

"And history has shown that not to be true," says Mrs. Kinkade firmly. "Not all who refuse orders to kill are traitors. In fact, some who have used obeying orders as justification for killing have been judged war criminals."

"When I think of being given commands to kill, I'm reminded of 'The War Prayer' or whatever that speech was called. The one by our nation's most famous story teller. He never published it himself for fear of public sentiment," says Greggy. "How did that go? Oh, yes.

O Lord — our young patriots — go forth — smite the foe. Help us to tear their soldiers to bloody shreds. Help us to cover their — fields — the pale forms of their patriot dead. — to lay waste to their humble homes. — to wring the hearts of their unoffending widows with unavailing grief. — for our sakes, who adore thee, Lord.

"I guess I don't remember it that well. Still, that's part of how I feel about this war – about appealing to God for help in killing. I've read far too much lately about 'our' religion in the Joint Military Service Academies. And in Federal government Initiatives. Now some are talking about lowering the age for Forced Sacrifice. It seems to me that older and Exempt adults want to start sending children, especially poor children, off to fight in their crusade," finishes Greggy.

"T minus fifteen seconds and counting. T minus ten seconds – nine – eight – seven – six – five – four – three – ignition – one; and we have liftoff." Ibrahim and Neil are listening to a radio feed of the first critical minutes of flight of the target vehicle for the SDS final exam.

"It seems to be going well," Neil says. The first and second rocket stages have been spent and jettisoned.

"Upper stage engine cutoff. We have tracking showing course good, altitude good, and speed good," comes over the radio.

"That's all we need to know. The target is on the proper path to cross the scheduled landfall," says Ibrahim. "The system is expecting this first ever, programmed test. It can handle both the test and any incoming enemy Intercontinental Missiles at the same time. We are protected by SDS even as we validate the system."

Gregory talked to his friends from his parents' home that weekend. He found Micah chatting on the Internet. He told him about his Choosing and what was going through his mind. They met for lunch at a familiar restaurant near the Upper School campus they shared a short time ago.

Micah urged Greggy to double check everything.

"Before you make any irrevocable choices."

"I'm only given fourteen days to report for training, Micah. That's from the date of the letter. By the time I get back to work on Monday I'll have only eight days left. I can't find a war Essential job and hire on in that time. I will ask again, but I'm damn sure this job doesn't qualify."

"I understand," said Micah. "It would be nice to know the criteria the Sacrifice Boards use for Choosing, wouldn't it? I hear a bunch of old men make the choices in secret. Women are almost never on the Boards. No one knows if there is any consistency between local Boards. There are movements to try to pin this stuff down and make it more open. That won't happen in the next eight days though. Here, let me buy you another beer."

Micah left for home after telling Greggy he would "pray for world peace." He intoned it in mock seriousness as a joke. But it was a lousy attempt at humor given Gregory's position. He apologized and Greggy forgave him, but it didn't leave a good taste.

As he drives home, Micah thinks about other people he knows who might soon find themselves in Greggy's position. In fact, he has a date with one of them this very evening.

Raven had been right about Micah. Here it was, weeks after that lovely kiss in her driveway and just now, finally, they are going out on a first date. They've been together many times in groups, doing the things students do, but this will be their first real date.

Raven was about to give up on Micah ever finding the courage to ask. She was considering doing the deed herself when the call finally came.

"I called your parents' place and talked to your mother. She said you'd moved. I didn't know you'd do that," said Micah.

"That's 'going out into the world to be an artist' for you," said Raven. "Let me give you my new address."

Micah arrives on time. He looks great to Raven. They have reservations at a fashionable downtown restaurant. And both have dressed for the occasion.

"He may be a nerd but he's a good looking one," she thinks as she lets him in her apartment from the little common hall outside. Raven's building is not large, but she has one of the largest spaces in it. Only two such units share this floor and its landing.

"Would you like to see my new place?"

"I'd love to, Raven. You look beautiful this evening! How long have you been in this apartment? Are you painting and can I see what you've been doing?"

The kiss is long and decidedly warm. They both just fall into it after the 'beautiful' comment. He obviously means it, and she wants to show him that she appreciates it. Raven is glad she spent all that time getting dressed to kill.

"Well then, let me show you my apartment and Studio," Raven says. "It's not large but it does have enough space for me. And yes, I have been working. I will show you some of my work, but not everything is ready for other eyes.

"That's the little bathroom beneath us," she says as they ascend the broad steel stair to the loft. After inspecting Raven's bedroom, which overlooks her workspace; Micah tours the Studio. It occupies most of the space on the main level. There is a walkup kitchen on the main floor's interior wall. That's the wall with the bathroom behind it. The two longest walls and a third are all windows – from just above the floor to the bottom of the high ceiling.

"You've got three works in progress?" Micah asks. He is staring at the large covered canvasses on easels.

"Only two," Raven replies. "The largest one is my 'masterpiece'. I retrieved it from the school's Main Exhibit Hall. You've seen it before, haven't you, dear? I've just covered it to keep dust from settling on it. I don't know how long it will be before I have it framed and properly hung — somewhere.

"I've been painting cityscapes, Micah. I didn't realize, didn't look at, the glory of the skylines outside my windows when I first moved here. The histories some of the individual buildings tell; their relationships to the flow of the city, to its districts and formal monuments; well, they're in need of my painting them too. This is something new for me. I'm in love with living in the heart of a vibrant, important city for the very first time."

"Speaking of a vibrant city, our reservation for dinner is coming up soon. Do you think we should be heading over there now?" asks Micah.

"Not just yet," says Raven. "I've got a special wine for us to have a glass of first. I bought it just for this occasion. It will be the very first wine drunk in my new Studio. There should be a toast! Besides, it's a quick drive to the restaurant."

"I'll leave my car parked on the street. We'll take a cab," says Micah. "I noticed a stand just across the way. It should be easy."

Dinner is wonderful. Micah cannot take his eyes off Raven who, after all, intended it that way. Eating together while enjoying the ambience of the restaurant and chatting about things they have and feel in common – which now seems to be everything; is sensual and easy. And it feels like home. Micah brings up the question of forcedsac, both Raven's Availability and Greggy's Choosing, just once.

"I'm sorry for Greggy, I really am," says Raven. "I'm not too worried about myself though. They don't seem to Choose women nearly as often. Anyway, I've already rolled those dice. Now, that's enough of that for tonight. Tell me more about you, dear Micah. How do you like your new job?"

After dinner and the cab ride back to Raven's Studio there is the bottle of wine to finish. There are paintings to look at. The brightly lighted city is a fantastic backdrop to it all. And there are many more kisses. The two of them fit together very well, in many ways and at many levels. Micah entirely forgets to worry about his car parked all night on the street.

Alarms are going off. They have expected lots of activity at the consoles. But it's too early for this. There seems to be something wrong with the test mode settings. All of the alarms are sounding. That includes those that should be silent in test format.

"Radar data from the birds off the coast indicates a target approaching. It's at about the right landfall," says Ibrahim.

"It's too low that far from the coast, Sirs," says one of the uniformed Space Command technicians. "It's barely in range; but looks to be at about three hundred and seventy kilometres altitude. On a ballistic trajectory for the impact zone, at that distance out, it should still be over four hundred kilometres high."

"Something is wrong with the target," says Neil. "Initial readings on altitude must have been wrong. It's going to fall short."

"Can't we override those alarms?" asks Ibrahim. "They're going to trigger all sorts of responses we don't want. Automated

Emergency Messages will go out on the public airwaves soon if we can't shut them off. Damn!" Neil stares at Ibrahim. He has never heard Ibrahim swear.

"The system has gone into autonomous mode, Sirs," says the technician. "It's refusing to let us alter anything. And behaving as if a real attack is occurring. It's acting as it's supposed to when faced with incoming Intercontinental Missiles. The settings for a test remain. It still seems to be expecting that. It's almost as if — both the test and a real enemy target are being tracked by —." The technician's voice trails off.

"Get me central Space Command now. The Watch General Officer should be standing by on us. We don't have a choice. We must assume this is not a test," the uniformed Strategic Defense Systems Operations Chief says.

For the next five minutes everyone is busy verifying the radar data. First the target's position is determined by birds in the net. Then, as the target comes fully into range, ground units confirm that. The lasers on the birds that will engage the target first begin preheating.

"The target is coming in at a constant altitude. Damn — it looks to be in low orbit!" exclaims Neil as he views the projected course and altitude on a monitor.

"Sirs, we have a second bogey behind the first. It's smaller and higher. It's where the test vehicle was supposed to be," says the technician.

"What in the hell is this?" says the SDS Operations Chief, Colonel Tucker. He's staring at a fuzzy image displayed on a monitor. "Space Command just sent this recon over. It's from a satellite used for other — well, 'black programs'. Ones we can't talk about. They say they've been tracking this from over six thousand kilometres off the coast."

"This is not an Intercontinental Missile. Either from the other side or our own," says Ibrahim. He and everyone who heard the Chief have clustered around the console where the picture from space is displayed.

The spacecraft is hard to make out against the inky black behind it. The intense sun somewhere above the thing has overexposed the top. Sunlight reflected off the planet illuminates it only faintly from below. The photo is almost painful to look at.

The craft is unlike anything Ibrahim or Neil have ever seen.

"What do you think the big booms sticking out are for? says Neil. "This big circular thing looks like – a huge dish antenna."

"It's hard to really know the scale, but I'm guessing the thing is enormous," replies Ibrahim. "It's probably the size of one of our net's birds. It might even be as large as one of the monuments."

"It's no missile of any kind I've ever seen. It looks almost — alien — from somewhere else."

Chief Tucker speaks quietly into the secure phone for a moment and then shuts off the display everyone is staring at.

"A Profile Yellow condition has been declared by Space Command," he says. "All of you without that clearance are to leave this room immediately. You remain on duty. Report to the Auxiliary Control Room down the hall. Mr. Starks and Mr. Valentine, get back here. Both of you have clearance. It's shown by those yellow dots on your badges."

A room of over twenty Technicians quickly drains to a half dozen people. The Chief snaps a manual lock on the door behind the last person out. He then steps to the Classified file cabinet. He spins the combination dial on the bottom drawer. The one neither Neil nor Ibrahim have seen opened before. Chief Tucker removes a folder and opens it. He moves to the Primary Console, and begins pushing buttons and flipping switches. He consults a bright yellow page from the file. The alarms go silent one by one.

"Gentlemen, the test will be rescheduled," the Chief says. "Something more important has appeared on our radar screens."

20 THE PURSUIT OF HAPPINESS

Micah is lost in thought. He is reviewing the work of a colleague, an intern like himself though an undergraduate. The work is simple. Micah could have checked its accuracy from memory. But he must be sure it uses the same number of significant digits in constants, and the same letters to represent variables; as spelled out in the company's Design Standards Manual.

"Talk about 'pushing paper'," Micah thinks. It isn't the work that he is lost in. Micah is reliving his date and the entire wonderful evening with Raven.

Lovely Raven isn't just a good friend anymore. She isn't just a hot new date. Micah is falling hard for everything R. M. Winthrop is now and promises to be. He is thinking of Raven in his future. Seeing her at the core of that future. Talking with her during dinner and then, more intimately, as they lay falling asleep in each others' arms; Micah realized that Raven really is all the amazing things he thinks of her as. Micah knows that Raven has mastered the improbable part of self that he hasn't pursued. The daring part that he is too timid to go for. The beautiful and amazing Raven doesn't just awe Micah. She humbles him.

"It's as though she is the empty parts of me."

Micah enjoyed a privileged and happy childhood. Being watched over makes most healthy souls, as time passes and they become adults, long to be the watchers. Micah will soon celebrate his twenty-fifth birthday. One more year and he'll have completed all the formal education he has plans for. It's obvious that he can go out into the world and be successful doing what he trained to do. But Micah is thinking of more. He is thinking warmly of Raven and, vaguely, of a family life of his own – of their own. Micah is gathering the courage and words to ask this woman if she is having thoughts about a life with him too.

Micah's Lower School life was one of simple immersion. Childhood friends and he moved from schoolyard play to more serious study gradually. They hardly noticed the change. The harsh realities of the world were things read about in newspapers and seen on television. They had little actuality for the privileged and the truly loved.

That middle period in life that so many people complain about; the transitions in body and mind, in outward appearance and self image; flew by for Micah. He lived then mainly lost in books. He returned to people in the last years of Lower School. When cliques and emerging life interests began to decide people's paths and destinies.

Micah went out for some sports but was never a candidate to excel in any. He dabbled at school journalism and the written word, but knew he wasn't that keenly interested. And he was one who fortunately recognized how bad his poetry really was.

He tried some performing arts – both as part of a group, an orchestra, and individually. Music was fun. He lingered long enough to understand how deep it could go. But he finally wandered off. He found individual performance very self revealing. Those who could 'just do it' intimidated him. Micah was not one of them. He found his path, his future, finally, when he tried technical drawing.

When he put pencil to paper in mechanical drawing class, Micah recalled how much he loved to draw in school as a child. He began evolving a plan. One that put his abilities in science and math together with this controlled drawing to forge a future.

Now Micah is near acquiring his last credential as a highly ordered cog in the machinery that builds and services civilization's infrastructure. He is an engineer. But he recalls the childhood joy of coloring outside the lines. He sees amazing Raven; willing to entirely reveal herself Raven; and defining the lines and then coloring outside of them Raven as the freer spirit he longs to be but has not the brashness for. Raven stands in for Micah. Her fearless choice to go for the improbable makes him love everything she is that he is too frightened to be.

A new fear forces its way into Micah's dreams. As he pictures Raven in his future, he broadens his concerns for her happiness. Her vulnerability to forcedsac sounds an alarm.

There are ways even an artist can acquire Exemption from Forced Sacrifice. The obvious one is being classified as a Conscientious Objector to all war. This is by design virtually impossible to achieve. Except by Clergy of the 'right' religions. As far as Micah can tell, it exists only for Forced Sacrifice Boards to point to. They point to it as evidence that the law has considered individual conscience.

The 'out' for Raven that Micah keeps coming back to, short of fleeing the country, is open to all females. It is marriage and motherhood. Fatherhood garners no such benefit. Micah knows that both Exemptions for school and for motherhood have time limits. If the war goes on long enough, both he and Raven could be Chosen. Just as Greggy was.

Micah finishes reviewing his coworker's paper. He throws it in his Out basket with a hastily scrawled 'Looks good' on the routing slip. It's time for lunch. Micah heads for the sandwich shop he frequents on the main floor of this enormous building.

While he waits for his food, Micah watches a news bulletin on the TV mounted above the bar. NSEA believes that the probe to the planet on the far side of the sun has gone into orbit there. It's possible that disaster or disasters unknown have befallen the spacecraft behind the sun's disk. But the fact that it has not reemerged at this time leads to certain knowledge that a simple flyby mission hasn't occurred. There is cautious optimism that an orbital survey of the sister planet is in progress.

21 FROM ON HIGH

"Your attention here, please. Specialists with advanced expertise will be joining us shortly. While we wait for them, I will brief you on what we know so far about this — spacecraft," says the SDS Chief, 'full bird' Colonel Tucker. He switches on the monitor he had shut off. This displays again the fuzzy picture of the unlikely craft against the backdrop of oh-so-empty space.

"Few people know that the Strategic Defense System was designed with dual capabilities," says the Chief. "The primary mission of the system is to defend our nation against attack with Intercontinental Missiles. But shortly after serious design began, SDS received a second mission. This is an extension of the detection and tracking that are part of the defense function of the satellite net.

"The system was designed to look down on the world to see ballistic missiles. They tweaked it to work with other high orbit satellites to also look out. To spot threats to our world from space.

"In the last few decades, visual observations and then satellite tracking of asteroids – space rocks big enough to pose real danger to our world – have alarmed scientists," he continues. "We used to believe the possibility of collisions with these rare objects was so tiny as to be dismissible. It turns out they are more common than that.

"Geologic investigations have shown that the planet has seen significant impacts. Some of them have happened quite recently, as measured on a geologic time scale. These have changed our world's physical nature and its life forms' destinies. SDS can help us foresee and possibly prevent having our life forms drastically altered by a random event from on high.

"Obviously not a space rock," says the Chief. He is pointing to the unlikely image on the monitor. "However, it did come into this low orbit from a much higher one. Space Command tracked this 'probe' dropping from an initial apogee of about forty-eight thousand kilometres, to its present planet skimming height. It did that in just a few transits of the globe.

"A 'black program' satellite took this picture at about six thousand kilometres off the coast. Only that low orbit bird has passed close enough to image the probe in visible light. Our satellite did a radiological scan too. The probe carries no weapons of significant power. Space Command has decided to just watch what it does as it passes over us – for now.

"This probe has shown capabilities for the other side that we didn't know they had. They might have launched it into a high orbit and then redirected it to this low one. Or it might have originated somewhere high above the planet. The reason for this orbital game is unclear.

"The probe appears equipped to transmit vast quantities of data. Note the enormous radio dish here. We estimate the probe's size at twelve metres across, from projecting boom tip to boom tip. It's enormous. Larger even than the spacecraft in our net. Are there any questions at this time?" the Colonel finishes.

"Launched from 'somewhere else — above the planet'. Where?" asks one of the technicians. He has a puzzled look on his face.

"We don't know that. It's possible that a very high orbital platform was used to 'drop' the probe into low orbit," says the Chief. "Another suggestion, one I consider highly unlikely, is that the probe was launched from a lunar platform. Either scenario might have been used to confuse the origin of the probe, or for some as yet unknown purpose."

"A lunar platform — do you mean a moon base?" says Ibrahim. He is clearly skeptical. "Nobody on this planet has that kind of capability. Even we have never soft landed a lunar probe. Our research money goes to the necessary buildup of military space systems. Because the other side does the same."

"Not a lunar platform — that we know of, certainly. However, as I've said, this probe proves that capabilities we did not know the other side has do exist," replies Chief Tucker.

"Suppose it's not from the other side. Or from any 'other side' on this planet?" volunteers Neil Valentine.

"Let's not get ridiculous, please," responds the Colonel, looking sharply at Neil.

"Colonel, Sir, look at that thing. It doesn't look like anything I'd dream of designing much less try to launch into space," says the technician. "If you built a fairing big enough to house it for launch, you'd be talking a twelve metre diameter rocket."

"We'll have people here to assess what we know soon, son. In the meantime, I'm not going to speculate on how it was launched," says the Chief.

"The people coming are apparently trained to assess rocks, Colonel," says Neil. "This is clearly not a rock. And it appears to me to be well beyond any capabilities known to exist on this planet."

"Now, I'll have to order you to resist more speculation of that nature, Mr. Valentine," says the Colonel. "If you do not shut up, I will have you arrested by the MPs. I'll be forced to rely solely on Mr. Starks's knowledge of the system."

Neil Valentine shuts up. He knows that to continue may be dangerous for himself and for his family. Full Colonels and up are vested with the authority of Motherland Security. And everyone has come lately to know how great that power and authority is.

22 MOTHERLAND

They rolled all of the old intelligence services into what had been the Department of Homeland Defense. They renamed it the Department of Motherland Security. The Chief Executive made this change. He made it just after he and his new Minister of Security were elected. The Chief Executive is known as the Commander in Chief to the military.

The Ruling Class was tired of the Bureau of Investigation. They were tired of the Intelligence Agency too. Both of them kept on offering Intel and analyses that diverged from Executive Policy. And 'The Chief' wanted to use the BI and the IA as he chose: without quaint geographic restrictions.

The Commander in Chief wanted to use the military's Intelligence units as he chose too. The solution to all of this was simple. The Chief created a new Junta-level post. This allowed one person, a company man, to run them all.

Before there was Motherland, silly rules to prevent the government from invading citizens' homes and persons prevented this efficient merger. Motherland swept away fears that a heavily armed and rigid military might invade people's lives on some whim from on high. Motherland also broke the intelligence branches' insistence on presenting Intel just the way they saw it.

And then new Justices invigorated the Top Court. These were men who were sure that there is no right to privacy in the Revised Federal Constitution. The Court saw to it that the people had no recourse in the matter.

And so, the country was properly 'fixed'. Like a pet that has had its spirit and drive, its reason for daring the improbable, cut out by a selfish master.

Being quite aware of this new reality, Neil Valentine quits talking. He quits to protect that most dear to him: his loving wife and precious children. Neil might have continued to speculate had he only his own freedom to lose. He has always been outspoken. But Neil knows they are imprisoning people now for what used to be called 'free speech' and 'free press'.

Neil knows that torture is now Executive Policy in some places. He knows that his country's military punishes men suspected of being on the wrong side there by arresting their wives and children. The soldiers that guard the entrance to Neil's place of employment are from that military. Neil is unhappily, suitably cowed.

Afraid to speak, Neil recalls a quote from one of the country's founding fathers. He said that those willing to give up essential liberty for temporary security were deserving of neither. Neil remembers a favorite teacher's assertion that people who use the words 'security' and 'peace', but seldom mention 'freedom', are likely hazardous to all three.

But Neil must comply with the Colonel's order. He has the nerve to speak out. But Neil's reasons for being – the children he is raising to be a better future – are threatened by forces he cannot resist alone. He vows to help vote the bastards out next time around. He will undo the damage done.

Neil recalls another phrase uttered by a Founder at his nation's birthing.

"A Republic, Sir, if you can keep it." Of course, that was before they declared the Federal Empire.

23 THE CHILDREN'S CRUSADES

Monday dawned far too quickly for Gregory. He had driven back to his own apartment late Sunday evening. He didn't want to. But he knew he couldn't get to work on time in the morning, leaving from his parents' place. He forced himself to shower and dress and then made the short drive to work. He spent about an hour absently sorting through his In Basket. He reviewed what he thought would be his schedule for the week. Then Gregory walked down to the Personnel Department. He found the person in charge and asked the single question on his mind.

"Does, or could, my job qualify as war Essential by any definition of the term?"

"No, Mr. Kinkade, as you were told when you hired on. Your job is not on the list of Essential positions approved by the government for this office of the firm. Have you received a letter advising you of your Choosing?"

Gregory was unprepared for this question. He considered lying, but knew they could, and would, check with the military on his status.

"Yes. It came in Friday's mail."

"I will advise your immediate supervisor, Mr. Kinkade. You will want to talk to her or him as soon as you can. There are no open Essential positions at our location. It will take you a couple of days to formally check out. So, do not delay. And do not hesitate to ask us for any assistance you need in departing."

Gregory walked slowly back to his office and sat down to think.

"That happened fast," he mused. "They're obviously programmed as to procedure upon hearing the 'good news'. Unless I hurry, I won't have time to use the few contacts I've made here to check on Essential positions elsewhere in the company. I must do that before I'm pushed out the door."

The ringing of his desk phone interrupted his thoughts.

"Mr. Kinkade — Gregory, please come see me in my office," said his supervisor.

"Well, if I'm going to arrange transport out of the country, I will need a couple of days to put my affairs in order. Without a job interfering," Greggy thought. He walked glumly down the corridor between the cubicles belonging to his new but soon to be his old coworkers. He knocked and then entered his supervisor's walled office. He knew he was about to be given a timetable for his leaving.

Raven Winthrop sits looking out the windows of her Studio at the busy thoroughfares of the capitol. They stretch to the horizon. There are parks scattered about the landscape along these broad ways in every direction. Majestic alabaster, pale pink, and champagne colored monuments reside here in the large green spaces. They are in the middle distance and beyond.

Directly below Raven, the scene is more commercial. There are shipping facilities, a truck storage depot, and distribution centers on all sides. Even this architecture is handsome though. The buildings are well designed. They show classically inspired details.

It's late afternoon on a Monday. The sun is infusing the scene with the rich golden hues it acquires shining low through the thick, particulate laden air of the big city. Raven is working on a cityscape looking northwest from her building. It's on one of the large canvases she had in her Studio the night Micah came to her, already weeks ago.

She has sketched in the buildings, streets, and monuments that tell the story R. M. Winthrop sees. She has begun painting these in bright colors. Raven adds shading and details, including pallet knife applied texture on some of the nearest pavements. She brushes a wash over the coats of paint to change their character to this yellow afternoon's warm and lazy tones.

Raven takes a break to think about what she is creating. She steps out into the common hall to retrieve her mail and returns with it to her walkup kitchen. Raven Michelle sits at her breakfast, lunch, and dinner table examining a curious sheet of stationary. She removed it from the first envelope she opened. The letter begins with a one-word salutation above a few harshly block-formatted paragraphs. 'Greetings', it says.

Baruch has absorbed his religious training well. He has made what he learned into his life, as his teachers told him he must.

"You are a devout man," the Revered Scholars who are his teachers tell him. Baruch has studied carefully the other information those same teachers provided him. His efforts to fabricate explosive devices to combat the evil foreign troops, to drive the devils from God's own land, have also met with success. Some of his weapons already have been usefully employed.

"Now it is time for you to go from here, from your training ground, to do the work. This is God's Holy work. For which you have been prepared," says his Revered teacher.

Baruch and others from his class are to move to the frontier near the border with the large nation that provides them with support for the resistance. There they will make arrangements on certain roads to prevent the evil soldiers from far, far away from reaching the border with their war machines. They must do this work within three weeks. Baruch asks why. His Revered teacher tells him it is better if he does not know – at least not yet.

"Baruch, we do not leave for a week," says his Teacher. "You are blessed that your father lives but a short distance away. Do you want to visit your family before you go to your first great task, and possibly to your reward?"

"I would like to see my father and my family again," says Baruch. "Now my father and I will speak more as equals. I am sure my mother and three sisters would welcome my presence. I wish to talk with my brother as well. Can I leave now? When must I return?"

After packing his few clothes, Baruch begins the day's walk to his father's house. He goes determined to return in pure service to the Only God. To face whatever God determines as his fate with courage and understanding in his soul.

Gregory finished by noon on Wednesday. He signed a form stipulating that the matching savings plan funds from the company he had been so excited to work for would never be his. He hasn't been employed long enough to become vested in them. He signed to stipulate that, by withdrawing his own savings plan funds, he is subject to a big Federal penalty. He must withdraw his own money because he is terminating his employment. And that penalty might be larger than any interest paid to date.

Gregory stipulated that he has been employed less time than required to receive sick or personal time pay. His last check will be short any such pay already made. He stipulated that, while the law guarantees his job upon his return 'from lawful conscription'; the company cannot guarantee that "— this job or an equivalent will exist at that time. Here or at any company location." Gregory signed many more damn stipulations. All of these benefit the company or the Government. None of them benefit Gregory.

Greggy had his exit interview on Wednesday. A personnel person from the company that had been so happy to hire him asked questions. And Gregory answered them. Personnel seemed smug when it asked him what his plans were after leaving the firm. As if Greggy could have any plans now. With the Federal Government calling the shots. Personnel implied that it was absurd that Gregory should find himself in this situation. Greggy had to admit, in hindsight, that it was absurd.

There was an awkward lunch in the break room. His now former colleagues wished him well in his future outside the firm. His supervisor asked Gregory if he had removed all his personal things from his cubicle.

"You are encouraged to leave before the close of business, even though we will pay you for the entire day," his boss said.

"And that early out gift is from my now former supervisor," Greggy thought. He handed his company ID badge to a guard and walked out the front door for the last time. Greggy carried his belongings in a cardboard box beneath his arm.

Gregory had spent Monday night in his apartment. But he felt so alone and down after all of Tuesday's stipulating, that he went back to his parents' place. He stayed in his old room the night before his last day on the job. He was late to work after driving from there across town to his final day with the firm he'd been so

117

excited to work for. Nobody had noticed.

Now Greggy sits in his car. He has already removed the company's parking decal from the window. There is a One Day Temporary parking pass thrown on the dashboard. He is trying to decide what to do. Suddenly everything in his life is cardboard or throwaway. Only his Notice of Choosing seems to have substance.

Greggy doesn't have to go to his own apartment right away. He hasn't lived there long enough to collect much of anything. Much less living things that might need care. He knows he can move out in a few hours using the old, faded blue truck in his parents' back yard. The lease he signed is bound to be another damn stipulation, but so it goes.

Thinking about fleeing – fleeing his life – Greggy remembers the words to an old song he heard years ago.

"Freedom's just another word for nothing left to lose."

He decides to go back to his own place, where he can be alone to think about all of it one last time.

Baruch enjoys the walk home in the dry heat of the bright sunlit day. This is his land and the land of his fathers. He revels in its familiar clear sky, warm air, and long views to the horizon. Surely the evil soldiers from far, far away have no such home. Perhaps this is the reason they are trying to take God's land from him. He will discuss it with his Revered father this night.

Baruch knows his father will question him when he tells of his mission to the frontier.

"I will tell him only that I am instructed to go and do God's Holy work," he thinks. "I need tell my mother, brother, and sisters only that I am well and doing the things my Revered Teachers tell me I must do in service and worship of the One God." And that will be the truth.

As Baruch enters the city of his birth, he sees that it is closing time in the marketplace. He hurries to his father's shop where he finds him just leaving for home. His father greets him warmly, with satisfaction at seeing him so well.

That evening, after worshipping in the familiar Temple with father and his brother, Baruch enjoys the family meal and family life. He enjoys it more than he thought he might. He has been so busy with study and worship these past months, that he drove thoughts of home from his mind. At least, he told himself he had.

Raven knows almost immediately what the coarse, terse letter is. But she studies it closely as if it might prove to be something else. Or there might be an 'out' to find in it somewhere. It is what it is though and starkly so. Perhaps that's why there is so little of it. It's intended to cleanly cut off all hope. Raven has "— fourteen (14) days from and including the date of this notice to report for duty." They mailed the letter, or it was printed, five days ago. Now Raven has only nine days to decide what to do and do it.

"I have to plan and then I have to act – fast," Raven thinks. She crosses the room to her easel and begins cleaning brushes and putting away her paints. Perhaps for a very long time.

Gregory is not happy with his decision. In fact, he's not sure he has made a decision. But he has settled on a course of action.

"I cannot flee the country. It will ruin my life and possibly taint forever the lives of my family. It offers no guarantees of anything. And the possibility of ruin for any future I might attempt.

"I will accept the government's decision like so many before me. I will use my education to try to safeguard my life while in the service – as an engineer. If I'm lucky I will never hear the order to kill. I might never even carry a gun. I might not serve in the war zone. I took my chances when I didn't go on to graduate school and accepted a non-Essential job. This is the hand I have been dealt."

Gregory spends some time calming himself and further rationalizing this path. Then he drives to the family home. It is midafternoon when he arrives. The house is empty. He pours himself a large drink and sits down with paper and pencil. He lists everything he must do to meet the Joint Military Services' scheduled report date, Monday.

He calls the Transportation Services number from the last paragraph of his Notice. He learns that the last commercial flight with military priority that can get him to his Training Base before the deadline leaves Capitol Airport Sunday morning.

"If you are not on this flight or on an earlier priority flight and are late arriving at your Base, you will be assumed a fugitive resisting Forced Sacrifice. A Warrant will be issued for your arrest."

"Thank you for that information," says Gregory. Now all he must do besides move out of his new apartment; store his new belongings; arrange settlement of outstanding bills; and close ongoing accounts is to explain all of this to his father — and to his mother.

Baruch's few days with his family are soon at an end.

"Be careful, my son and always go with God's Holy Word," his father tells him as Baruch prepares to return to the Religion School. His mother cries again. She has cried often these last days.

Baruch does not feel so strongly today that this is his soul's answer to the call. His mother told him that neighbors including a boyhood friend died while he was away. Explosive devices intended for the evil soldiers killed them. Baruch does not know where the devices he built were used. The possibility that it was here disturbs him. He will ask a Revered teacher when he gets back to school. Surely his teacher will know.

"Be careful of the streets, brother," Baruch tells the other remaining Akheron son. "Stay away from vehicles and away from soldiers. Stay away from everything and run when you must use the roads."

Baruch wishes there was more he could say to protect his brother, his mother and sisters, and his Revered father. Waving and putting on a determined face, he leaves his family again; perhaps for a very long time. Perhaps for the last time.

"This will not happen to my daughter!" Markus Winthrop, Esquire roars. His voice rises in defiance. "I can have you employed as a Page in the Chamber tomorrow, Raven. Let me protect you. I will see to it that your job is war Essential. You can go on with your painting nights and weekends.

"Perhaps working for the electorate will do you some good, daughter. It might even make you think of serving the people yourself someday. More women are going into government all the time."

"Raven, do not do this my dear," begs her mother, Nancy. "It will haunt you the rest of your life if you go to prison. It may seem noble to you now. Maybe it is. I don't know. But it will not seem that way to people you'll want to hire you or appoint you or even elect you in the future. It may not seem that way to the man you want to marry someday. Listen to me, Raven. This is not a good choice."

Gregory's entire family helped him vacate his apartment and move his new furnishings into his old room at home.

"It will all be here waiting for you, son, when you get out," says his father. His mother puts on a brave face. She has argued and cried so much that her voice is gone. She nods her agreement with her husband. Greggy's family drives him to the airport. They wave goodbye as he walks down the concourse with his single suitcase in hand.

ALL WE ARE GIVEN

BOOK 8

Bob, Weave, and Conform

24 THE PROBE

Three soldiers with yellow dots, and red dots, on their ID badges and carrying large aluminum briefcases arrive at the building. Front desk Security announces them to Colonel Tucker. The Colonel unlocks the SDS Control Room and lets them in. There are salutes all around. A Master Sergeant leads the group.

"Well, let's see your current tracking of this thing then. Where is this surveillance photo from space I have yet to see?" demands the Sergeant.

"Not an asteroid," he proclaims as he gazes at the monitor. "And we're sure this thing fell into low orbit from on high? How do we know that?"

"That's what Space Command told me," replies the Colonel. "You would have to talk to them to get details. They didn't give them to me."

One of the Lieutenants in the trio exchanges a nod with the Sergeant and a "By your leave, Sir" with the Colonel. Then he gets on the secure phone to contact Space Command. It's clear that these men are used to close teamwork.

"While we wait to get the latest information on this, I'll tell you what has been determined and decided so far," says the Sergeant. "You've probably all heard that this probe looks to be incapable of major physical mischief. Its nature is almost certainly pure surveillance. It seems well equipped for that. Notice the booms — here, here, here – and here, I guess. We think they are likely to house sensors of some kind. Maybe cameras separated by as much distance as possible, to improve stereo imaging. Or things we haven't thought of – yet. After analyzing its flight path, Space Command has decided to let the probe take a few more turns over our landmass.

"Here's the curious thing," the Sergeant continues. "The other side knows from years of surveillance pretty much where all our Intercontinental Missiles are. It's likely this probe is not on the path it was supposed to be on. Unless it does some fancy maneuvering, it's not going to see much from where it's at. Except a few of our cities and some pretty countryside.

"Existing missile emplacements and the new SDS ground assets are well beyond its field of view. Or they are in some way shielded. We think it's an enemy operation gone bad. It's a real opportunity for us to understand what those bastards' space Intel capabilities are.

"I wouldn't be surprised to see them take their own ship down," he continues. "When they can do it without us having a chance to look at any wreckage that makes it to the surface. It'll pass over us sixteen times a day until then. It's only in range of our best sensors, here on the ground, about fifteen minutes of each orbit. We've got to make that time count. If everyone works hard and pulls together, we can make their mission our mission.

"You will probably be allowed to shoot the probe down to complete the Operational Test of SDS," the Sargent says to Ibrahim and Neil. "If the bird is still in orbit when we've got all we can from studying it. Oh, one more thing. You are mistaken if you are under the impression that my group is only trained to assess rocks."

The three open their aluminum briefcases. They begin pulling out miniaturized state of the art electronic equipment. They've brought a few documents too. With the Colonel's permission, they plug the flashy equipment into sockets and jacks on some of the SDS Control Stations. Including especially the Primary Console.

"What is all of this, Neil?" asks Ibrahim. "I don't know what equipment is intended for these interfaces."

"Neither do I," Neil replies. "Some of these ports are marked 'For Expansion' on my Coordination Drawing. Some of them are unmarked. It's a classified drawing. The original has a higher clearance than I can see. My copy has been altered and reclassified for my eyes."

The probe carefully assessed the sister planet as it neared it. Far from Dr. Mariam's and the NPCO team's watchful eyes, artificial intelligence weighed and measured the target. The probe found its mass and its atmosphere to be similar though not identical to the home world's.

The planet's axis of rotation is not perpendicular to the plane in which it goes around the sun. And that axis points always at one spot in the heavens. The sister planet has seasons.

The trace on the ground of the probe's path orbiting in that plane will oscillate north to south as the tilted planet rotates. From an orbit just outside the atmosphere the probe will see a wide swath of the planet. Its trace on the ground will shift or precess to the west with each circuit of the globe.

The probe used the planet's mass and distance from its star to compute its path. It made the calculations for orbit. Then it performed a final course correction engine burn. Later, a long braking firing slowed the craft dramatically as it closed in on the planet. A short and precise burn put the ship into an elliptical orbit. It ranges up to an apogee of forty-eight thousand kilometres above the planet.

From this close distance, the probe measured the planet's parameters with greater precision. Then it began the switch to a nearly circular orbit. A few hours later the improbable probe was skimming the planet above an almost familiar atmosphere. It can see everything on the ground in a four hundred kilometre wide belt.

"I'm surprised it's still up there," says the Sergeant. "After three chances to learn something as it passes overhead, we don't know much more than when we first photographed it. Space Command says its estimated mass is too large. No rocket could have boosted it off the planet in one piece.

"That's why a launch from a high platform or a lunar launch was proposed. They could have assembled the probe from pieces. They launched the pieces separately. Then they dropped their finished probe from a platform. Or they flew it from a moon. It could have appeared in low orbit almost magically.

"Intercepted transmissions from the other side say they think it's ours. I'm sure that's a ruse. The self destruct mechanism must have failed. Or I think it would already be gone."

A technician answers the secure phone and hands it to the Sergeant. After some discussion, the Sargent hangs up and turns to the group.

"Okay. We've got a decision to allow it one more day's fly time while we try something the boys in lab coats have dreamed up. Space Command is not worried that the probe's path is getting close to reconnaissance targets of worth. The other side has already seen the missile silos that are now coming into range. The new SDS emplacements are still not within its sight. We get this additional time to analyze the thing. But we need to move fast.

"Space Command is going to illuminate the probe with ground based lasers," says the Sergeant. "They say that analyzing the reflected light will allow them to determine the materials it's made of. This is like using a spectrometer to find the elements in stars by examining the light they give off.

"The probe doesn't give off light. So, the light must come from an outside source. Just one laser's single-color beam is inadequate for this. They will use every wave length or color of laser we have that can reach the probe through the atmosphere."

Arranging the laser firings will require a day or more. The firings can then take place over at most a few orbits. Ibrahim is interested to hear that the monument ships in his net will be receivers for the reflected light. This reminds him of how little he knows about these few and unique birds. And the equipment the Master Sergeant's team connected to the SDS control consoles surprised Neil. There are aspects of this complex system that its two greatest experts are not experts on.

"We'll control the monument ships' sensors from this room," says the Sergeant. "The instruments we've connected to the Primary Console will let us do that. Now, we've got to wait until equipment is set up at the laser sites. We're going to continue monitoring the probe until then with just this one, need to know crew.

"None of us leaves the facility. We'll have cots brought in for us to sleep on. There will be no communication with anyone outside this room. Colonel, Sir, would you please designate two teams? Separate both Mr. Starks and Mr. Valentine and yourself and I into different shifts. We need to have both system expertise and military command in each group. I believe eight hour rotations might be best."

Everything is ready to go twenty-eight hours later. Preparations to fire five super high power lasers through the light scattering atmosphere, with precision aiming, are complete. They await only the target. The lasers are in five locations. Engineers have checked and rechecked their calculations. They need to be sure that satellites with capable sensors will be in positions to sample the reflected light. The great altitude of the few monument ships and their locations make additional receivers for the light critical. They will also use some better positioned but less capable black program satellites.

They had to move one laser hundreds of miles inland from its coastal location. A satellite parked over the east coast will receive the light reflected from its shot. Some of these lasers' owners are not government institutions. The military has had to persuade them to lend out their lasers.

The next time the probe crosses over the only superpower, four of the five lasers fire successfully. Reflected light 'hits' are recorded by three monument ships and by some classified number of black ones.

"We'll catch the fifth laser on the next orbit or the one after that," says the Sergeant. "The probe's precession requires that we recalculate when to fire, but those equations are now in the computer. It won't be hard to do."

The people tracking the probe get surprised again. The probe begins changing its orbit. By the time it clears tracking from the east coast, it looks to be shifting to a transfer orbit. It switches to a polar path. When the next opportunity to fire the tardy laser occurs, there is nothing to shoot at. They spot the amazing probe over the western ocean. It is moving from south to north along the 'ascending node' of a polar orbit. It is out of range of anything based on the superpower's continent.

"It will only take a few tens of lines of code," the senior programmer said. "The possibility may be small but it is still real. If there is life on our sister planet – intelligent, capable life – they might be able to track and even interfere with our probe. We should program for that.

"We've made a list of dangerous events. We can change orbit to move away from that danger. A programmed series of engine firings, with their lengths calculated by the probe, can move it to a polar orbit. From there it can continue, if necessary, to avoid the part of the planet that posed the danger.

"We should also program the probe to cut the mission short and leave orbit with the information it has, if attack comes from too many places. Make that several tens of lines of code — a couple of hundred lines — at least," she finished.

After days of discussion, they decided to give the probe the ability to recognize an agreed upon, negotiated list of attacks on itself. They gave the probe with artificial intelligence the ability to choose to evade those attacks or to flee the planet. They increased the probe's active computer memory size yet again.

One danger sign is light in a narrow range or 'band' of frequencies. The ruby red wave length of weapons lasers is at the center of this band.

Wave length and frequency are two ways of measuring the same thing. As wave length increases, frequency decreases. Long wavelengths are at the 'red', the low frequency, end of the band people's eyes can see. Short wavelengths are at the 'violet', the high frequency, end. Beyond either end are 'colors' that people can't see.

People sense longer 'infrared' wave lengths as heat. Some animals and cameras can see infrared. All of these are forms of electromagnetic radiation. Some other EM wavelengths that people use are microwaves, X-rays, and television and radio wave bands.

"Well, this new orbit will bring the probe over our landmass in time as well," says the Sergeant. "The path is precessing. With each orbit, the north to south part of the polar orbit, the 'descending node' or dragon's tail, comes about twenty-three degrees closer to our east coast. We've got about six hours until the probe is in position for the laser's beam to hit it. And satellites are in place to catch the reflected light. Engineers are still confirming those calculations.

"Space Command was surprised by the change in orbit. They believe it proves there's a high platform of some kind we have yet to find. A platform to relay data from the probe and send instructions to it from the other side of the planet. Otherwise it was coincidence that the probe changed orbit right after we fired at it. I'm not a big believer in coincidence.

"Some have said that there is another possibility. But that would require declaring a Profile Red. And that's not going to happen.

"The lab has come up with another test to run while we wait for the probe to line up for our laser," continues the Sergeant. "We won't be directly involved in this, but we'll continue to monitor the probe once it's again in range of our space and ground sensors.

"On a new topic, arrangements have been made for each of you to make one phone call outside the facility. With monitoring of course. To let your families know that you're all right. Nothing is to be discussed about why you are still here."

"Motherland Security will be doing the monitoring. So be damned careful what you say," says the Colonel. "I'd hate to lose any of my team at this time. To say nothing of the civilians that might need to be detained to suppress knowledge of what's going on here."

Nobody in NSEA was sure just how much probing the amazing probe would tolerate before it decided to run away. Computer algorithms make up the self protection function. Multiple copies of each of these are linked as nested subroutines. Some scenarios the programmers devise suggest that the probe will never flee. Or that it might flee at the first hint of trouble. That makes the probe's responses quite possibly like those of a biological brain.

They decided to give it a test consisting of a half dozen likely scenarios. To see how it might work in some real world. To see if the idea is even wise. The biological brains decided that the electronic brain passed the test with flying colors.

Preliminary results from the unfinished laser study come out while Space Command waits to fire the last 'light cannon'. Much of the probe appears to be made of low density carbon. This might be a graphite-like material. And they have found aluminum, which is also lightweight. A new estimate of its mass puts the probe within the single launch capabilities of some heavy lift rockets.

The probe comes into range of the only superpower's landmass again. Space Command starts 'scanning its EM signature'. After a couple of passes subjected to this assault, the probe seems to react again.

It stays in polar orbit but alters its path to move back over the ocean. It is out of range of the nation's land based equipment. When ships begin scanning it from sea, it disappears. The last known trajectory of the amazing probe shows that it has left orbit and is headed for deep space.

25 MARCHING AS TO WAR

Gregory arrived at the airport deep in the nation's heartland along with some new friends he made on the airplane. Nearly half of the passengers in the tourist section of the commercial flight were to-be soldiers, conscripts and enlistees. After a few conversations, they began seeking each other out among the civilians also riding in the cheap seats. Camaraderie is quick to develop between people sharing a small space and fear of the unknown for four hours.

"Military passengers should disembark and proceed to Concourse B and the doors there to ground transportation," said the pretty voice on the plane's intercom. "You will be directed by military personnel along the way. We hope all our passengers have enjoyed this flight and that you will consider us for all your future air travel needs."

Gregory wished he could have spent more time chatting with the stewardess whose voice he recognized on the plane's speakers. He talked with her earlier, when she spent more time than needed serving him drinks. He knows they'd both enjoyed it. He asked for and she gave him her phone number.

"It's likely the last time I'll get to see her. There are far too many people and things I may never see again after vanishing from my life for two years – or more."

Gregory heard on the plane about the military's Stop Leaving orders. Enlistee or inductee, after your time is up, they can simply decide to keep you because they don't want to lose trained personnel. The government can keep you, apparently, just as long as they choose. Regardless of what the papers you signed say.

The odd little airport amused Greggy as he walked down an ancient stair from the plane's door to the tarmac. There was no Jetway. Only this aluminum thing on wheels that they have pushed up against the plane. They parked the big jet a long way from the smallish terminal. You must hike to the building.

Gregory crossed the old asphalt-patched concrete runway in the dry desert air. He watched the baggage truck drive into a fenced area within the airport. It pulled into an open-air facility with a cover like a big carport. The handlers began unloading suitcases on the high side of a metal-sheathed, slide down ramp. The ramp was as long as the baggage truck.

"That must pass as a carousel here," Greggy thought. "I assume that's where I go to get my suitcase after entering the building."

Military Police wearing fancy chrome helmets and black armbands met the conscripts and enlistees where they entered the concourse. The similarly dressed MPs at Capitol Airport had answered questions from the to-be soldiers while directing them to their planes. The MPs here were blunt and more standoffish. These recruits were nearly to their Training Base. It was time for them to begin the transition to bulk war materiel and lose their identities as individuals.

"Step out through that door and find your gear, recruit," an MP told Gregory. "Then walk right, to Concourse B, where you will be directed by another MP." Greggy exited the doors at the end of the concourse. These lead to the baggage area. The baggage crew has closed and padlocked the gate to the runways. Greggy sees that three ribbons of razor wire cap the high fence.

Outside the door from Concourse B to ground transportation sat a drab military bus with its doors open. There were bars on the bus's windows. The MPs in the Concourse here merely pointed when approached and said nothing. Outside, two silent MPs wearing side arms stood near each end of the bus. They flanked both sides of the door from the terminal. Someone had hung a paper sign above the bus's door. It displayed a phrase Greggy had heard somewhere before. Abandon Hope All Who Enter Here, it said.

Greggy met his Drill Sergeant. The DS taught them the basic rule of "absolutely, immediately, and without question." Gregory got a Government Issued uniform and a shaved head. Finally, they marched to the barracks or bunkhouse.

There was a long lecture by DS about what did and did not go on in 'the bunk'. And about the schedule of training that would "— commence immediately." Gregory learned that the next day would consist of written tests, physical exams, and inoculations. Followed by an afternoon of drilling. Wake up is at 0500 hours. First assembly is in front of the bunk at 0515.

DS told the recruits that "Due to the need for troops at the war, the usual eight weeks of Training will be compressed to four weeks." After which Gregory can expect to be deployed "— wherever the service needs you.

"Listen up, civilians. If you work hard and learn what I teach you, I can make you into soldiers in four weeks. I am the only man on the planet who can save your worthless lives."

After twenty minutes to eat dinner and a lecture about the Base in general, it was 'lights out'. That time in the Mess Hall was all Gregory got to exchange a few words with his friends from the airplane. The ones that he could find. It all went by so fast.

Greggy thought as he was falling asleep about the banners he was looking at when the lights went off. The ones hanging in the dark above the bunk's doors to the outside world. The banners that say God is on Our Side.

The morning was easy, really. Greggy is accustomed to waking before dawn. The fight by thirty men to use the bunk's bathroom in fifteen minutes was ugly. Mess was fast. Greggy realized it always would be. "Eat and don't socialize."

Gregory is used to taking tests. The inoculations were the only real pain to the physical exam. Like everything else he'd encountered so far in military life, it was fast. After a fast lunch it was drill time.

"Today we're going to see what you've got. We're going to start building you up into soldiers," said DS. "Half of you punks are all flab. We'll take that off and put real muscle on you. The other half of you worthless recruits could blow away in a good wind. We'll put muscle on you too. You're going to hurt – bad – for most of the next four weeks starting now. Don't even think of telling me you can't. Don't ever stop doing what I tell you to do until I say stop. Do what I say to do absolutely, immediately, and without question."

That night in the bunk, a Lieutenant Colonel, a Chaplain, gave a speech to the recruits.

'Greg', as he was "— to be known from now on, recruit," hurt so badly he had to fight to look interested and remain standing at parade rest. The Chaplain's speech, which was really a prayer, ended like this.

"Oh, Lord, we go forth to smite the foe. Help us to tear their soldiers to bloody shreds. For our sakes, who adore thee, Lord."

By the weekend Greg had lost most of the terrible pains in his muscles and regained the feeling in parts of his body. Most of his aches now were low-level background ones. Greg was used to it. And he was beginning to like it. It reminded him of the physical prowess he was gaining. Greg could do three times more pushups now than he had ever done before. He could tell he was running faster and had more stamina too. He had learned to take apart a rifle and put it back together in short order. And he was making his own bed for the first time. These last two accomplishments he cared much less about.

Soon weapons training would begin in earnest, DS said. While DS yelled and cursed at his 'worthless recruits' the whole week, Greg could tell they were beginning to come together in formation. They were marching and presenting arms nearly as a single entity. Greg wasn't sure what good would come of that. But it made more sense than getting his bunk's bedding so tight that DS could bounce a coin off it.

"There will be no passes issued this weekend. Every one of you worthless recruits will remain on post," DS said. However, there would be a movie one night. Not a GI hygiene film but real, if old, entertainment. There would be some free time to write letters and to read.

"If any of you are up for a friendly basketball game, this bunk is authorized to use the gym on Saturday," said DS. "Other groups will be in there too. We encourage friendly rivalry between bunks. Just make sure you win one for me."

"I think I can manage three more weeks of this," thought Greg.

The Training Base is part of a larger Post that houses soldiers all the time. Whether there is a war on or not. There are thousands of soldiers here working regular jobs. They live both on Post and in nearby civilian apartments and houses with their families. A lot of what these soldiers, many of them lifers, do is receive, renew, and ship out equipment for war. There are hundreds of acres of land here devoted to storing the big weapons of war – vehicles, tanks, artillery pieces, and the like. There are tens of huge warehouses for the smaller stuff.

The equipment comes in from and goes out to bases around the planet. It's good to have stuff preplaced in case wars break out somewhere far, far away. They rotate the equipment of war for maintenance and repair. This keeps it serviceable past what would otherwise be its end of life.

A big Post like this has competitive drill teams, marching bands, and sports teams to put up against other big Posts' teams. Friendly competition, between Posts and between bunks, helps build camaraderie.

When Greg enters the basketball court, he sees the team roster, the retired jerseys, and the slogans for the Post's basketball team on the walls above the bleachers. They hang over the doors to the outside world too. The slogans over the doors say in large, bold text: The One God Roots for Us, and We are God's Own Team. Gregory wonders how that can be. Considering that he met recruits on the plane who worship different Gods than his. He begins wondering exactly which One God all the signs are talking about.

Before lights out on Saturday night, the Chaplain comes to the bunk again. Gregory knows now that there are several Chaplains of different faiths and sects at the Post. But only this Chaplain visits the bunks and makes speeches that are really prayers. He is the highest ranking Chaplain. At the end of his prayer, after the bit about tearing enemy soldiers to shreds, comes the invitation to Sunday services.

"I hope to see all of you in Chapel at 0700 sharp tomorrow morning. Be sure to come at 0700 to hear my sermon – the real sermon. God expects you to be there. I'm sure your DS will second that after I leave you this evening." And Greg's DS did second that.

The next week was more of the same except there was more target practice with the rifles. Heavier weapons entered the mix. Greg didn't mind the mortars too much, although he felt sure they would ruin his hearing. But he resented the land mines instruction right from the start.

"There is something innately evil to hiding an explosive for an unsuspecting person to stumble on. And then be blown to pieces," thought Gregory. "The bomb can't distinguish between a soldier, who should be suspicious and wary, and a kid just playing with his friends."

He recalled that the most powerful country on the planet, his country, wouldn't sign a treaty to stop using land mines. Because the most powerful nation wouldn't pledge to go along, the treaty signed by nearly every other nation did go into effect. But it didn't have much impact.

Greg went to the real Chaplain's service his second Sunday on Base. DS made it clear that life would be easier for Greg and other holdouts if they went. Listening to the 'real' sermon made Gregory realize that it wasn't just which One God you worshipped that mattered. Which sect's practices you adopted in worshipping that One God mattered too.

Gregory knows that some politicians think this proselytizing in the military is wrong. And they demanded a law to stop it. The government passed a law with a title that sounded like it would strengthen separation of church and state in the military. But the law really made it easier for people like the Chaplain to press their sect's beliefs on recruits. Regardless of which god they worshipped or how they worshipped which god.

When he heard about the law with the misleading title, Gregory remembered a phrase he'd heard in a class while discussing propaganda. "Tell the lie as though it is a most important truth."

Gregory's third week in Training involved more long hikes with heavy packs and more frequent trips to the obstacle course. What DS had said about putting muscle on his recruits was true. Now they all showed the impressive results. Weapons training continued nearly every day.

The obstacle course grew a 'live fire' section where recruits sometimes made mistakes and died. The course added a simulated town that recruits had to storm and 'clear'. It was obvious what part of the planet the town depicted.

Greg and most of the recruits in his bunk got their first passes their third Saturday night at the base. Gregory didn't go to town. He stayed on Post with those who "— have not earned the right to leave their Training even for a moment." Greggy wanted to spend the time writing another letter to the stewardess from the plane.

The real Chaplain came to the bunk that afternoon, before the men with passes could leave. He repeated his prayer and his invitation to worship. He made sure the men leaving for the evening knew that the real God still expected them to come to His sermon tomorrow. Greg knows that few now bother attending services other than the real one. And he knows that those who stubbornly follow their parents' and grandparents' ways had better go to both.

"Of course, those who wish to worship in other ways will be accommodated. Those services will be at other hours on Sunday," the real Chaplain added.

And Greggy recalled: "Repeat the lie until it is believed to be the truth."

Greg and most of his bunkmates get their Assignments early in their fourth week of Training. The Orders that tell each recruit what Unit they will be joining and where they will be going in the world will be issued later. The Assignments, which are based on the written tests of the first day, tell each recruit what kind of work they will be doing. Greg's Assignment is as an engineer – a Combat Engineer.

"I'm going to use the few days left to harden you recruits as much as I can," says DS. "Where most of you are going, 'hard' will be what saves your nearly worthless asses. There will be no more time off in town. You cannot afford that waste. Those of you who did not get passes last time should pay strict attention now. That was a wakeup call. If you do not wake, you will soon likely be dead. You should pay attention if you want to have your best chance to survive as soldiers."

Gregory wakes at 0500 on Sunday. He makes assembly in front of the bunk at 0515 sharp. When he returns from the real

Sunday service, he finds his DS waiting with Orders for everyone.

As he hands the envelope to Greg, DS says, "Here you go, soldier. Remember what I taught you and best of luck."

BOOK 9

Those Bastards

26 THE LION AND THE LAMB

Micah is having lunch again in the pub on the main floor of his office building. The restaurant with the old-fashioned brass trimmed and mirrored bar is convenient and comfortable. It serves good lunch fare along with what looks to be an interesting assortment of beer and liquor. Micah would like to come here for drinks some evening when he's in the city. But the place is only open weekdays and not very late. He has imagined bringing Raven here after the theatre to show her where he works.

Micah has been thinking of Raven a lot since their date. He knows he should be asking her out again – soon. However, he's still sorting out how much of his soul's longing he dares reveal right away.

A suddenly loud and flashy News Bulletin on the television over the bar interrupts Micah's thoughts. The probe to the sister planet on the other side of the sun "— has reemerged from behind our common star. No data has been transmitted yet, but the carrier EM signal from the spacecraft has been identified."

Micah has avidly followed the mission's news. Including especially technical details about the probe. He knows that the date for the probe's return depended on how much it could see. The probe decided when and why to fly home with what it has learned. Micah knows that the probe's time orbiting the sister planet was supposed to run longer than this. He is immensely curious as to what the probe will reveal and why it is returning so soon.

"We will have further Bulletins as more information becomes available. We hope to release detailed photographs of our sister planet from close range soon," says the announcer. The unremarkable program that was interrupted resumes. The sound volume drops. And Micah returns to his thoughts.

Micah has been thinking lately of all his friends, not just Raven. He's been thinking of their school days and children's lives now ending. It has been weeks since Greggy entered military service rather than following his own choice to refuse an unjust and immoral war. It startles Micah to realize that Gregory's Training might already be over.

"How long has it actually been? Micah wonders. "Where is Greggy? Is he still practicing marching and awaiting orders at his Training Base in the heartland? Or has he shipped out to somewhere not nearly so safe and comprehendible?"

Micah hasn't heard from Greggy since their lunch together before he left to train. That was when Micah made that terrible joke about praying for world peace.

"Is Greggy holding that against me? What a stupid remark it was." Micah isn't overtly religious, but he says a little prayer in his head for Greggy. He hopes for dispensation for his friend, and for himself. As granted by some undefined higher power.

That night Micah finally decides he's ready to call the beautiful, amazing Raven and ask for another date. He intends to slowly reveal his feelings while trying to gauge Raven's heart. Micah is prepared, however, for a headlong rush to confession.

If it feels right – feels happily beyond rational control – he will simply propose marriage to Raven the next time he sees her. Micah knows he is in love and wants desperately to proclaim it to his chosen one. And he is willing to risk totally exposing himself this one time and just do it.

After trying repeatedly to get Raven at her apartment, Micah calls the Winthrop home. His call there goes unanswered, except by a machine. Micah leaves a message that he's calling for Raven and hopes she will return the call. He adds that he'll call again later. Later, he gets the machine again. He leaves a rambling message asking Raven for a date any time of her choosing and hoping that everything is going well for her and for all the Winthrops.

"I'll call tomorrow if I don't hear from you," he finishes.

The Winthrops don't have live in servants. But Micah is used to a family member or someone from their staff answering the phone when he calls. He has never heard Markus's somewhat pompous phone 'greeting' before. Not getting a live voice, twice in one evening, leaves him a bit uneasy.

"Out to a play, the opera, or some political function" Micah reassures himself. "Just my luck. Now I'm even more delayed in talking to her. Why did I wait so long? I'll be sure to call early tomorrow."

Raven and Nancy, a couple of their employees, and Markus have spent most of the day and well into the evening removing Raven's things from her Studio. They moved them to the suite of rooms in the Winthrop mansion that has been Raven's home since her birth. It was much easier moving out, with a myriad of Raven's friends helping, than it has been moving back. Each Winthrop has had the thought during this long day that hiring a moving company might have been a good idea.

Raven is amazed at how much new art equipment she has acquired, along with some used furniture, in less than two months on her own. She refused to allow her parents to pay for this move on principal. Raven herself could not afford professional movers. It's bad enough that she had to beg for and accept a loan grudgingly offered by Markus to pay off her lease. Raven had no choice in that. It was well beyond her own means.

Going to Markus gave him another opportunity to persuade Raven to accept his plan to keep her from Forced Sacrifice. And to allow her to remain in her cherished Studio. Her father's offer of a war Essential job as a legislative Page tempts Raven. But she has made this decision based on her personal integrity and the fact of her Choosing. Raven is willing to bet her future on her moral positions regarding this war and forcedsac. She is betting on the improbability of right defeating might.

"Micah has called twice while we were moving, Mom. I want to talk to him but I don't know how to tell him what has happened and what is going to happen."

"You and he are a couple, aren't you, Raven," says Nancy.

"You need to tell him what you're going through, dear. You need his support and he deserves to know about all of this."

"How about a late-night snack as a reward for our labors?" asks Markus. He has walked into the servants' kitchen and interrupted Raven and Nancy's discussion. "Let's sit in the breakfast nook and have a family conference. I promise not to bully anyone. I just want this family, together, to understand where we are and what is going to happen next.

"I love you, Raven. It's difficult for me not to be the protective parent. However, I also respect you as an adult. I know I haven't always made that clear. I need to tell you about my realizations concerning the importance of your chosen path in life. I think I finally understand just how amazing, unique, and important your talents are.

"Come on. We're all alone now that our loyal staff members have left," says Markus. "Let's get something decadent out of our refrigerator in the big kitchen. I'll brew some tea or coffee. We could even open a bottle of wine, if that's more to your liking at this late hour."

The Winthrops sat up late unwinding from the rigors of the move and the stress of the gathering storm. They talked as a family of loving parents and adult child. They came to necessary understandings about where each one stands on the issues. Raven made her parents understand how important her beliefs about Forced Sacrifice and this war are. Her parents impressed on their daughter just how grave the consequences of her planned defiance of the government might be.

It was the kind of exchange this once larger family, short now two fully independent and flown children, hadn't had in a long time. It made Raven remember how much she loves her dad. Nancy recalled how wise her husband can be. And Markus realized how much his strength depends on these two women. Who are now his primary and really his only emotional support.

They all agreed that Raven has the right to defy forcedsac and still receive her parents' support. And Markus has the right to use all the power he can conjure to protect his daughter. In every way that she does not object to. Markus vowed to use his daughter's Stand, with her permission, as a goad to the public's conscience regarding the Leadership's dirty war. And its 'with us unquestioningly or you're the enemy' stance.

It is the right and the responsibility of every citizen to speak out against what they feel is wrong in their government's policy. Especially if it violates the law. They all agreed on that. Nancy's love and calm guidance saw them through to the shared conclusions they needed to reach. On some points they could only agree to disagree. But even in that there was understanding and respect.

And Raven told her parents about Micah. She revealed how deep her feelings for him are. She made sure they understood that he too is now an important part of her life. Markus and Nancy impressed on Raven that she must let Micah know of her intention to refuse forcedsac. And to pay the consequences in a very public fashion. By the time they were ready for needed sleep, family bonds had been strengthened. And all had steeled themselves for the public debut of Raven's Stand.

"This is almost beyond bearing," says the soldier in the narrow, slung webbing seat. He is sitting next to Gregory in the big military transport plane. The plane has no interior finishes to speak of. The soldiers sitting with their backs against the plane's shell can see its aluminum 'ribs' and skin. There is no insulation between the soldiers and the outside. It's cold sitting and waiting for time to pass. Lashed-down pallets of gear nearly fill the broad central aisle made of unfinished aluminum planks. The aisle runs the length of the fuselage. The plane has no windows to the world.

"We've been flying for nearly twenty-five hours now," replies Greggy. "We've had a couple of stops where we could rest our ears from the drone of those four big turboprop engines. I hate that we can't get out of the plane to stretch our legs. I hate that walking the length of the fuselage, threading our way through our gear to the head at the rear of the plane, is our only exercise. I don't even know where we stopped."

"If we're on schedule; and that's a big 'if' when talking about the military; we should be near our final destination," says the other soldier. "We'll know for sure when we hear the enemy missiles exploding around us as we descend to our landing. If we're lucky enough to hear them."

"You will be alright. We will be all right. Together we will bear this and whatever else we must in the next two years – or whatever it takes. Until the end of our days or we go home again. Whichever comes first. Now — let us pray for world peace," says Greg the soldier, with a wry smile on his face.

27 THE ONE(S) TOO MANY

A truck lets off Baruch, over a dozen of his fellow Religion students, and the youngest Revered teacher at a crossroads. From here two major dirt tracks take different routes to the country's northern border.

"We must make both of these roads to the frontier impassable to the usurpers' war machines," says the Revered teacher. "Guard your triggers and fuses. Without them the weapons we fashion from the explosives we are about to receive will be unable to cleanse the world. The Martyr's body belt and the Holy hand grenade must ignite to illuminate society everywhere. And to destroy those who will not see. Half of us will take each road. We will travel a day north before we begin planting devout death for the infidel soldiers from far, far away."

Baruch is glad the Revered teacher comes with his group, while the oldest student leads the others off. Now he will have a chance to ask about the first weapons he fashioned with his own hands. Baruch would know where those weapons were used. And whom they killed. The day is warm and the path is dusty. They guard their water and use it sparingly. They are unsure when they will get more.

After the early morning has passed and the sun and hot air have become oppressive even to those used to this land, they meet a large truck coming from a small connecting road. The teacher hails the driver and all wait while the two talk guardedly. The students get into the covered truck bed and the journey north continues.

There are boxes and barrels of materials in the truck that the students can easily fashion into bombs. The students know this from their studies. These will become the 'devout death' they bury at the roadside. They will be lethal surprises for any who come this way behind them.

Dusk is beginning to fall and still the heat of the day lingers when the truck finally stops. It has been good to be out of the sun beneath the camouflage tarp that is the truck's cover. But the air inside has been heavy and hot. Few have been able to sleep on this long journey. Now all help unload the truck's contents upon the sand. Baruch is glad to see that they are near a small group of trees surrounding a water hole.

They move the Holy war materiel to the shade beneath the trees. Then they brush the marks created by the moving out of existence. The truck leaves. The teacher directs the students to hide its tracks back to the road. Soon one cannot see, from the road or from the air, that a cargo of death has been hidden at the oasis.

"I cannot tell you, my son," answers the Revered teacher when Baruch asks about the explosive devices he fashioned to defend God's land. "I know they were used by moral, devout men who wished only to serve the One God. No one can tell where they were used. We do not identify grenades, Martyrs' belts, and bombs as being from somewhere or made by someone. We would not have the enemy know by examining them where to look for the makers."

Early the next morning they begin fashioning hidden death to plant in the road. The Revered teacher divides the students into two groups. He speaks with each group in turn before they begin the Holy work. He assures them of God's rewards for their efforts.

As each group completes its weapons, they set out up the road to hide them under the soil at the road's edge or directly in the road. They equip each bomb with one of two types of triggers. Where a bomb goes depends on its trigger. They space their devout death about one hundred metres apart, more or less, along the road. Sometimes they place their improvised explosive devices much closer together.

By the time one group has finished burying their weapons, the first students from the second group have made their way to the far end of the hidden bombs. The second group continues extending the line of death while the first one returns to fashion more bombs.

By the end of the second day, the journey to the far end of the line has grown to nearly two hours time. The explosive material is almost gone. All can see that they will finish on the third day.

Baruch adds a hidden touch to the last few weapons he makes. He stamps his initials into a metal strap that is part of the trigger mechanism.

"I don't know why I do this," Baruch thinks. "Surely nobody can trace this back to me or my school from two letters carved in the metal. The weapon's explosion will destroy the marks. Regardless of that, I do it because I can. I feel the need to. Only I will ever know of it."

"We have hidden from all but God, including even ourselves, where His weapons are. Now we will bury the boxes and other evidence that we have been here," says the Revered teacher. "We will brush the oasis clean of our tracks and cleanse the sand behind us as we walk back to the road. We will walk the road south in the dark of night. If someone finds us by tomorrow's light, they may be unable to tell even from which direction we have come.

"You must never tell anyone what we have done, on pain of death and despite torture. God willing, our surprises for the evil usurpers will seem to have appeared from thin air when they explode and do His Holy work."

The controversy over a high profile Representative's child defying the Leadership and the law changed. It turned into a religious argument in certain circles. The Leadership's political support includes a core of people who claim to be morally superior to everyone else in the world. What these compassionate but concerned conservatives pin their moral credentials on is difficult to understand. They are always first to squeeze the poor to pay for the excesses of the privileged class. Despite the tenets of the religion that they claim to be the models for.

Hucksters who take money from others with get rich quick schemes litter these people's ranks. They offer these ploys in their conservative and oh-so-appropriate 'think tanks'. They offer them in their churches and on their sanctimonious web sites too. These moralists' opinion of those who have no 'rightful estates', those who must struggle to earn their way, can be summed up by a line from a well known novel.

"Then let them die and decrease the surplus population."

These people are true to only one tenet. That is, 'If it can't be reduced to dollars and cents it has no worth at all'. They place no value on people and other living things. It reminds one of the joke where an attorney questions a plaintiff on the stand.

So, Sir, you accuse the international firm I represent of the wrongful death of your mother. Yet you admit she had weaned you before she died. Can you show this court any actual damages?

The President and the Prime Minister count themselves among these saints. They leap on Raven, brave soul and champion of the people's rights. They attack her for her Stand against deceit, theft of the people's resources, and mindlessness. The argument these sages wield is that they see Raven, a lion, as a traitor to her religion. They see her as straying from their version of the only 'right' religion.

Raven is clueless in this. She never considered religion to be a part of the contention. Raven's only religion is one she feels inside. It's about service to her fellow beings. And about caring for the amazing and beautiful world she gets to live in. Raven cannot fathom how she has won a subscription to a specific god's liturgy of death. Without having entered a contest.

Raven called Micah late in the afternoon of the day before she plans to refuse Forced Sacrifice. She had let him leave phone messages without replying for a full day. Raven wished Micah would just appear at her parents' home demanding to know what was going on. Micah would have got that desperate eventually. But his reserved nature kept him from doing so in a mere twenty-four hours of uncertainty.

"Let me come and talk to you," says Micah. "We'll go someplace private and discuss what you're about to do, Raven. I won't try to talk you out of it. I don't understand why you won't take your father's offer of an Essential job and save yourself from doing this. But I will support you in whatever you decide you must do."

"Dear, dear Micah; we both know you'll take my father's side. I've had a hard time not bending to the easy path he offers. I'd love to see you. I have some important things that I want — no, that I need to tell you. Come and take me, but let's talk only about us and our future beyond this war. Promise?"

It would have been easier if Raven still had her apartment. In the end, because it's early evening and he knows it is still open, Micah takes Raven to the pub in the building where he works. In a booth in the back they talk. Micah tells Raven how much their last date meant to him. He apologizes for taking so long to call her. Then, to the surprise of them both, he asks her to marry him. There in the corner booth of a tavern and without a ring to offer. He promises her one the minute the stores open the next day. And Raven accepts him as her to-be husband.

"I don't care about the ring. You can get me one when it's convenient. It's you I want, Micah. I love you. You're the nerd for me."

Now all is revealed. Raven and Micah are happily engaged. Raven publicly declares her refusal of Forced Sacrifice. But the Induction Center figures out who her father is and tells her to go away. She does not need to surrender her person for days yet. There is nothing to say to her until then. The newspapers and television proclaim 'Raven's Stand'. It and Raven and Micah's engagement is 'all the news' in the capitol and beyond.

Gregory heard the missiles exploding all around as the military transport plane made its hasty descent to the battle-scarred runway. He heard them in the far, far away capitol. Where they are assuring Security, access to resources, and freedom.

And the One Gods' cheerleaders – the Revered Scholars and Teachers; the soldiers' Chaplains; and the warplane drivers' 'Sky Pilots' – still preach their truths. They teach them to students and to enlistees and to conscripts alike.

28 US BASTARDS

Greg's Commanding Officer in the Combat Engineers is a First Lieutenant. He's a young, self proclaimed lifer named Charles.

"Call me 'Charlie, Sir'," he tells his men. "Except when we meet in public other than in the field, or in front of other officers. Then, of course, you will answer to me with 'Sir, yes, Sir' at all times."

'Charlie, Sir' soon becomes just 'Charlie'. Except when it might be overheard. Engineers are close team players. They don't want to bother with military protocols that disrupt their thoughts and waste time.

Charlie has several roles in this melee. He and his engineers must keep the machines of war working. They also build and repair bridges and other means of moving men and equipment. And Charles is a scapegoat if things go wrong for officers with combat troops in their charge.

Charles is an easy going officer. He views the personal weapons his engineers are issued as hindrances to the work. Something they don't need but must drag along anyway, like military protocols. His men see their guns the same way.

Charlie understands and accepts it all. He, like his men, is an engineer. He's one of the interchangeable cogs that ensure civil life and its infrastructure. Or, if orders call for it, that maintains war's access to the field, and its machines of death. Charles is a good soldier.

Greg finds out that there is a military Chaplain here too. His speeches which are really prayers vary little from those that Greggy heard in Training. This one might have been the first Chaplain's mentor – or his student.

There is a new and powerful dynamic added here. Soldiers on patrol in the incredibly dangerous city or its countryside sometimes do not return. Except in bags. Sometimes they come back in more than one bag, or box, to a soldier.

This Chaplain has something immediate and personal to use in His sermons. He points to the death and cruelty all around them as proof of the righteousness of their mission. Some have already leapt into the abyss. And they are all standing in a line, waiting their turns. Surely this makes them right and the enemy wrong. And those who will not see this are surely the enemy.

Greg sees that the divide between soldiers who go to the right Sunday services and those who choose other worship is larger here than back home. The horrors they see and participate in here scare many of these soldiers nearly to death. Those who didn't think about seeking the comfort of a higher power at home become regular worshippers here. And they want to attend the services they know. Those are the services of their parents and grandparents.

Far, far removed from the relative sanity and freedom from prejudice that was home; the forces of righteous conformance run free in this place. They single out and ridicule soldiers with the wrong religious convictions here. And their superiors force them to participate more often in the most dangerous tasks. Their lives are valued less. So, they are always 'on the line' and at risk of death or worse.

Greg sees all of this first hand while on patrol. Some of his first sorties involve clearing roads at the edges of the capitol of improvised explosive devices. The insurgents who planted these intend the IEDs to kill the evil usurper troops from far, far away. The insurgents are likely those men seen standing in tight groups in town. They are always talking low.

The bombs Greg and his fellow Engineers defuse are crude but effective. And the soldiers first over the bridge or down the road to discover and mark the IEDs; are most often those who worship the god of those who inhabit this land.

"They're uncivilized religious fanatics who have got their hands on modern weaponry. They will destroy civilization to ram their damn religion down our throats," Charles declares. It is dark outside. The Engineers are in for the night. They are staying in a defunct hotel. Only the men under Charlie's command are present.

"We've got to wipe them, like a stain, from the globe," Charles continues. "God will not allow us to fail. These infidels will kill us all if they can. We cannot leave one of them or one of their children alive, who believes in something other than the real God."

Greg is walking slowly down a dirt road far from the capitol city. He is still in the nation where Security, access to resources, and freedom are being assured. But the Engineers have moved north to probe the next, much larger country's defenses. In preparation for a full-scale invasion. It's oppressively hot under the splendid sun beating down through the clear sky. A sky free so far from the soot, stench, and smoke of war. Greg is thinking of home and of his last letter from the pretty stewardess on the plane to Training Base.

The Engineers have been walking down this road forever it seems. Greg is uncomfortable, bored, and discouraged at how little time has passed and how much remains of his 'tour' here. He swings his foot idly at a small piece of metal in the road.

"I shouldn't —" flashes through Greg's mind. But the heavy military boot has already met its target. And that is the last thought Greggy ever has.

"Oh my God, they've killed Gregory!" shrieks his mother, collapsing into her husband's arms. They are at the front door of their nearly fashionable suburban home. Two men in dark military uniforms are standing outside on the porch, on the other side of the screen door. Behind them there is a drab military sedan parked at the curb. The back doors of the sedan have no handles on the inside. And neighbors who have noticed the suspicious car in the double cul-de-sac, dead end court are looking out their front doors and windows. They are saying little prayers in their heads. Prayers for their neighbors, prayers for themselves, and prayers for all the children.

BOOK 10

Not Us

29 AT THE COROSSROADS

The Revered teacher's group rejoins the other half of the students at the junction with the second road to the frontier. Two of the students who took the second road are not among those returning south.

"One of them made a mistake. I do not know who it was," the oldest student and leader of this group tells the Revered teacher. "Both were working in haste to finish one of the last Holy weapons when it exploded. We were in danger of missing this meeting. We buried what we could find of them with the crates, barrels, and other evidence that we had been there. We said prayers for them, Revered teacher. We prayed as we walked away. I did not know what else to do. I only hope God will welcome them as the Martyrs they so fervently wished to become."

"You did what you could. God will not accept them as Martyrs. They did not die in battle with the usurpers. However, they were devout men and doing His Holy work when they died. I am sure they have received their rewards."

After the students return to the Religion School there is much meditation and prayer. Both for those who went out to do God's work and safely returned, and for those who still wait their turns to leap into His service. After some days, the Revered Scholars call Baruch to their council. They ask if he would remain at the School or follow a calling from the Scholars. They want him to serve as Prayer Leader at a Temple nearby which recently lost its Leader to an act of the war.

After prayer and considerable thought, Baruch decides, recalling the respect the Prayer Leader commanded at home, that he will follow in that mold. He will serve the One God in a way he knows his Revered father will welcome. Baruch learns after making this decision that it is his home Temple that needs the new Leader. There is more prayer and public dedication to serving the One God in all his needs. Then Baruch packs his things. He starts the short journey back to the city of his birth.

30 KID GLOVES

"Welcome, Prayer Leader," says the old man that Baruch recognizes as he who attends the Holy Temple and assists the Leader.

"God be always with you, Master of the Temple," replies Baruch. "It pleases me to find you well and awaiting me. I am sorry at the death of the Leader before me. Tell me, how did he die?"

"It was a bomb in a car, Leader Akheron. Some men parked the car in front of the Temple. He went to have it moved. It should have been me to go. I will regret for the rest of my days that it was not I instead of him. It is a loss for all of us at this Temple and in God's Holy society. But we welcome you, Prayer Leader. God is great. You will encourage us all in your new position, God willing."

Baruch unpacks his few clothes and some prayer items. He puts these into the closet in his room. He walks about the Temple, seeing it with new eyes. This magnificent space of God's is now his to shepherd.

"Between me, the Master, and some Deacons of the Temple we will care for this place of God. I will help pilgrims from afar and worshippers from the city alike to exalt the One and Only God properly. And in accordance with His Holy Book," thinks the Leader.

Leader Akheron leaves his Temple for his father's house. Evening prayers were over before he arrived in the city. There is still time to have dinner with his father's family. If they will have him as a guest.

It was rumored among those involved that a 'black bird' in high orbit spotted the probe speeding into open space. There was no physical trace remaining to prove that the enormous, almost alien craft had orbited the world. The photograph and the analyses of the probe disappeared into classified space. The need to know crews and scientists were forbidden to talk about it. No one ever printed or broadcast a word about it to the public.

The Press briefly noted the light cannons' firings and movements about the country. They were "an experiment." One to determine the nature of the edge of the atmosphere more accurately. Neil Valentine and Ibrahim Starks prepared for a delayed SDS final exam.

Raven presented herself at the Induction Center on the day after her deadline to report for Forced Sacrifice. She was arrested. The Center's MPs detained her. When civilian Enforcement arrived, they took her into custody. Raven hadn't signed anything accepting Forced Sacrifice. She hadn't agreed to voluntary service either. The Center maintained she was still on the civilian side of the law.

While Raven, her parents, and Micah waited for the Agents to show up, reporters and photographers interviewed and filmed them all. The media had arrived at the Center just before Raven walked in the door.

The Induction Center treated Raven and her entourage well while they waited. Center personnel offered them food and a choice of things to drink. The Center made them comfortable in an office off the main hall. They saw to it that members of Raven's party were not unduly stressed by the experience.

Center personnel acted as gatekeepers with the media. They let in only one crew at a time for interviews. The media went away happy with their video for the evening television news. And with their interviews and 'candid' photographs for the Late Editions and the next morning's Special Editions of the newspapers.

"Well, I'm glad that's over with," says the Induction and Recruitment Czar. He is a bird Colonel attached to the Joint

Military Services' Recruitment Central Office. He has been visiting the local Center since Raven's first attempt to refuse forcedsac. Civilian Enforcement has just left with Raven in handcuffs. The media have removed themselves and their equipment from the building and its parking lot.

"It's amazing the treatment people get who are connected at high levels, isn't it, Sir?" ventures one of the Recruitment Officers, a Major.

"Our National Leaders' reelections are coming up fast," says the Colonel. "Concern and sympathy are to be expressed to expand the 'big tent' the Party represents. Even if some VIP's relative on the Other Side is spouting sedition during wartime. I'm glad that's not my daughter committing treason. I am sorry for Representative Winthrop and his wife. But the publicity and fresh note in the Press of this office's existence might bring in more recruits. It might bring them in both locally and nationally.

"I've been told to expect this election cycle to bring a real surprise. And to not 'rock the boat' in anticipation of that. I take that specially to mean play nice with the Press. You did well in calling up channel for advice and handling this affair with kid gloves. Now we can let the civilian authorities deal with the matter and walk away as the good guys."

Leader Akheron has become known and well regarded by regular worshipers and by pilgrims alike in a few short months. He reads regularly from the Holy Book to those who follow him. He encourages all to live in accordance with its very words.

The Leader is careful to keep the Book's basic tenets in mind. Baruch does not preach Holy War, for the Book does not speak of it. He never exalts the taking of life to purify society. But he believes all who do not worship the One God in the proper ways will not attain Heaven.

On Holy days Baruch leads groups of pilgrims from the town to the Temple. He leads them to a nearby ancient Shrine of his sect too. Leader Akheron accepts the responsibilities and performs all of the rites expected of a Prayer Leader. And of a Keeper of his sect's Holy Shrine.

"Leader, a truck with men in it has been parked in front of the Temple all morning," says the Temple Master one day. Baruch has just returned from a walk through the narrow and quiet neighborhood streets behind the Temple. "I think they are seeking workers for some purpose. They stop and question many of our local men," continues the Master.

"They should not remain so long in front of God's Temple," replies Baruch. "I will ask them to move to another place."

As the Leader approaches the truck parked on the large street which dead ends at the Temple, he sees that it is now empty.

"I shouldn't —" flashes through Baruch's mind. He recalls how the previous Leader died. He turns quickly and begins climbing the steps back to the Temple and away from the suspicious vehicle. Men with nasty-looking guns appear from buildings on either side of the Temple. Baruch does not hear the shot that kills him.

The men pump many bullets into the still form lying crumpled on the Temple steps in a pool of red. They proclaim in loud voices for any who can hear that the One God is great. That a man who encouraged worship of the One God in the wrong ways is dead. That society must be cleansed of those who are sores and cankers upon it. It must be rid of Temples and Shrines dedicated to their wrong ways of worship.

After the destruction of the Temple, the people found the remains of two bodies inside. The attackers laid one of the bombs that brought down God's magnificent space on the ground near the bound body of what might have been the Temple's Master. Some claimed to recognize his clothes. No one could tell if he died before or after the explosives went off.

They found the second body near a rear entrance to the Temple. It was that of a small boy. It was impossible to tell who he had been. But the house of Akheron never saw the Prayer Leader's remaining brother after that day.

31 THE DARK SIDE

Sam's team, Mariam's people, and others unknown to them have been studying the photographs the probe took of the planet on the far side of the sun. They've been studying then for weeks. The pictures of events such as the shedding of the photovoltaic wings' covers are very clear. They provide proof of the big spacecraft's near perfect condition. The high resolution camera and data transmission system are working at top form. Everyone who helped build, launch, and support the monster craft is amazed that this almost far-fetched project is coming off so well.

They have released some photos to the public. These include unique shots of the next planet out from the sun. The probe passed by it at fairly close range. They have also released some of the most detailed pictures ever taken of the far side of their large moon. Its gravity helped sling the probe on its way around the sun.

The photos of the probe itself are the big hits in the Press. The Press has begun loudly asking "When will we get to see the close in photos of our sister planet? We want to see the photos taken from orbit."

Motherland Security and the Launch Complex have agreed that "Only distant photos of the Other Planet will be released at this time. And each photograph must be cleared before release."

Mariam and Sam and their people know why this is so. The Launch Complex's Executive Director, Dr. Jacobsen, has 'held for study' all of the photos taken from orbit. Even some of the shots transmitted before the probe disappeared behind the sun show something on the dark side.

Due to the positions of the sun and the target, the Other Planet's orb resembles a fat crescent moon in the approach photos. People can make out the curved margin and some detail on the dark portion of a crescent moon. And there is detail apparent on the dark portion of the Other Planet. The detail is revealed by traceries of light. These patterns look just like those in photos taken from space of the home world. When the lights of major cities and their connections are visible.

"Then they can go fuck themselves!" roars the Prime Minister. He wants to delay the national Leadership elections. But others believe that both the opposition and the Press will strongly resist that. "We have total control of the Legislature," the PM continues. "We can pretty much do whatever we want.

"There is a war on. This war is unlike any we've known. Enemy soldiers slip in and slip out of the populations we came to free. We can't distinguish them. We can't pin them down as one known political entity. They're not in one place we can bomb the hell out of.

"War calls for extreme measures. We cannot allow the Other Side to mismanage this war. We must maintain our control until we are victorious. We cannot accept any of that changing. Freedom hangs in the balance. And it's not just a matter of the terrorist threat. There is the war for control of the people's minds to consider.

"The Patrician Act is just beginning to give us the leverage to assure that only right-thinking people speak publicly and are allowed to govern," the PM continues. "The Other Side is full of people who think differently than we do. People who do not think right. People who would give away our position in the world. To achieve 'equity', 'fairness', and 'conformance to International Law'. Whatever in the hell those things are.

"I'll take another drink too, Mr. President, if you're pouring," says the Prime Minister. "I'd better call for a driver tonight. I can't have another DI conviction. And there's that too. We need to continue prosecuting the hell out of our war on drugs. Even if it sucks the treasury dry and leaves our grandchildren paying for it.

We can't begin to count on the fucking 'loyal opposition' to do that. Hell, half of them are probably smoking that damn crap. Make it a double, please, Sir."

The President, the PM, and the Secretary of Security and War have called a meeting with their advisors. They want to discuss the PM's Initiative to delay indefinitely the Leadership elections. The President has given permission for people to speak their minds. A junior member of the group, the Secretary of State Affairs, has voiced the obvious concern about a delay.

"I shouldn't have," the Secretary thinks. She recalls the former Secretary of State. He killed his career by speaking his mind one time too many. He was both a statesman and a military strategist. His military talents made the current Secretary of Security and War look feeble.

The Secretary of State Affairs wishes she had kept her mouth shut. She should have just listened.

"Speak when spoken to. Always agree with and submit to the boss. And just be glad to have a place at the table," she thinks.

"Well, Mr. Secretary, it's time to discuss that other matter. The one we need to keep among as small a group of minds as we can for now," says the Prime Minister.

"Yes," replies the Secretary of Security and War. "We need everyone else to clear out and leave this one to the grownups. No, Sir – Mr. President – you can stay."

"Here are the pictures of the other planet," says the PM. He takes large glossy photos from a folder on the table in front of him and spreads them out before the other two men. "It's like looking at yourself looking back at you in a mirror. There are people there, creatures of some kind anyway. They have the skills to create big cities like our own. Cities every bit as large and well lit as ours. I would have believed someone was trying to fool me except that — well, you can see the shapes of their continents. The city lights along their coasts define them. They are not Us.

"I'm told it's possible They tried to interfere with our probe. Telemetry says the spacecraft is functioning perfectly. But it left orbit early. It was supposed to do that if it detected a threat to itself. The fools who programmed it didn't arrange for it to let us in on what happened. All we know is that it's coming home early."

"The other planet looks to be similar to our own then?" asks the Secretary.

"Yes," says the PM. "We'll have more information on that soon. The Other Planet is close to our world in size and probably in composition. We're pretty damn sure the oceans we see in the photos are water.

"Their air is at least something like ours. Hell, for all we know They could walk around down here breathing our air and slaughtering us in our sleep."

"Is this another reason to not have the elections or a reason to have them?" asks the President.

"Sir – Mr. President, I can't think of a better reason to delay the elections than the discovery of a truly alien enemy. I'm sure the Secretary will concur with me on that," says the PM.

And the Secretary of Security and War does concur.

BOOK 11

Coming Home

ALL WE ARE GIVEN

32 ALL TOGETHER NOW

People assembled slowly for the meeting. They held it in the conference room where they grilled Dr. Baker for launching the probe to the Other Planet during the North Gate Incident. Sam Chakroborty and Mariam represented the launch team. Dr. Jacobsen was there for Launch Facility One's management. A dozen people wearing Visitor badges eventually joined them. Some of these people were wearing guns. These were revealed by not so subtle bulges beneath their suit coats.

"How did they get inside the gates with those?" wondered Mariam. New guards joined the regular ones Mariam thinks look so dangerous at all the Launch Complex's gates that day. The new guards were in dark military uniforms. They carried wicked looking automatic weapons. The regular guards didn't say much to the newcomers. They were too afraid of them.

"There is a new space program being organized by the Junta and the office of the Minister of Security," says Neil. "It's all very quiet and vague so far."

"I heard it involves putting weapons into space," replies Ibrahim. "Not defensive weapons like our little flock of birds, but weapons able to bombard an enemy from high orbit. Weapons that can obliterate cities and decimate entire regions without warning. I think our 'visitor' from space caused this. I hear that new rockets far more powerful than anything we have built before will carry

171

the weapons platforms into orbit. A crash development program will produce these in record time."

"How is it that you always know so much more than I do?" says Neil with an astounded look on his face.

The Strategic Defense System finally took and passed its last test. A rocket launched a vehicle designed just for this. It was launched along a known path toward a predetermined landfall. SDS found it and tracked it. The system hit it with kinetic weapons and killer lasers from the ground and from space. It did this while the target was in the 'cruise phase' of its flight. It was just outside the atmosphere and running silent. The test score was not perfect. Some weapons missed the target. But, overall, the system was judged a success. The only superpower in the universe should have been content.

"You should plead no contest and admit that you were influenced by 'terrorist propaganda' from the liberal press. They will let you go with a conviction pronounced by a judge. And with a couple of years' worth of probation. You won't have to serve in the military. Your conviction will bar you from that."

Micah is talking to his wife to-be, Raven. They are in a small Interview room with two walls and two sides that are prison bars. The bars open onto parallel hallways. People are listening to their conversation with hidden microphones. Raven's parents are waiting anxiously in the Visitors Room. They hope to talk with their daughter for the first time in a week.

"That's a felony conviction that will follow me the rest of my life, dear," Raven says. "It will keep me from doing many of the things I want to do in my life. Teaching is one example. I'll get the same conviction if I demand a jury trial and make the point that this war is illegal. That it is undeclared, and unauthorized by law. That's what will happen if I lose my case. If I win —."

"Everyone knows you can't win! interrupts Micah. "You might get lucky and win a first round with a judge who properly advises the jury to follow the law. But the government will bump the case up in appeals. Eventually you'll face panels of judges and no juries. The Presidential signing that altered the rule against 'double jeopardy' will let them do that.

"And those judges will be ones that the Leadership has been stacking the courts with since they were elected over seven years ago. Despite what the laws say, the only way to protest this war or anything else this Leadership is doing is to wait for the elections. And vote the bastards out."

They held Gregory Kinkade's funeral in a church near where he had grown up. The church was in a nearly fashionable section of a distant suburb of the Capitol. Some of those who attended were pleased that the funeral was held in this particular church. Some who came were barely able to stomach crossing this church's threshold. Some who knew Greggy but who worshipped a different One God could not bring themselves to enter this church. And authorities kept one, who believes the war that killed Greggy to be illegal, from attending the funeral for a friend.

They kept Greggy's casket closed. There was no viewing before the public ceremonies. Only Greggy's father saw his son after his body was flown home. He wished he hadn't.

The hearse that carried the casket from the church to the cemetery had a handle on the inside of the door in back. The government mandated the handle for safety. Soldiers in fancy chrome helmets fired guns into the air at Greg the soldier's internment. A Chaplain said more than a few words over the grave. They were words of inspiration for his family; encouragement that Gregory, the first Kinkade to graduate from Upper School, died in pure service to his country and to his God.

33 GETTING STRAIGHT

"Clearly we're looking at advanced civilizations on the Other Planet," said the man with a Visitor badge. He stood up in the front of the room. He seemed to be running the meeting. "These surveillance photos are so good that we can easily see weapons emplacements all over the place. Missile fields that contain tens of silos. The damn planet is armed to the teeth."

"But does that mean anything to us here on this planet?" said a woman in a pure wool business suit. The woman was wearing a Visitor badge and carrying a gun. "They're clear around the other side of the sun. Can they strike at us from there?"

"They have satellites in orbit," said the man. "They can launch large spacecraft around their own world. We didn't get enough Intel on those. The fools who programmed our probe only had it look down on the Other Planet's surface. We got lucky in spying one of their satellites orbiting just below us as we passed over. It probably got a good look at us too. We practically ran into it. It's likely they did something to provoke our probe to flee. We should go back, armed."

"This meeting was not called to discuss such things. There are civilian Space Launch personnel among us. We are here to decide what to tell our world about the photos, if we release even some of them. We have brought all of you including the civilians together here where it started to make sure we get our stories straight."

The man who said this stood up from the audience before he spoke. Everyone in the room looked attentively toward him. This included the man up front who seemed to be running this meeting, or Strategy Session, or War Council.

The war to secure the empire's life blood has gone on too long for the Ruling Class. The only superpower has an unarguable right to that blood. It is their 'clearly manifest allotment'. And there is a need for much more blood.

The superpower wants the energy reserves beneath the feet of a group of nations. It wants the energy to fuel its coming buildup in space arms. It's time to bring extraordinary measures to bear and finish off the war. Not only the Commander in Chief and his Junta, but also the Emperor agree. All say so publicly.

Talks at the highest levels resulted in a Finding. The probe that surveyed the only superpower was from the other side of this world. Or it was from another world. This shakes the foundations of the Federal Empire. Skills and technologies beyond those of the greatest power in the universe suggest there might be an even greater power somewhere. That must be remedied as soon as possible.

The only superpower can't fly to and orbit the planet's own moon, much less any place more distant. So, they make the practical decision. The superpower assumes the Visitor came from the other side of this world. They deny the possibility of an alien probe, a Profile Red event. This makes fixing the problem doable. Difficult, but within the realm of the possible.

Military Intelligence thinks the other side has developed certain technologies quietly. They might have a plan to counter SDS that involves this surveillance. They have a launch system that used Their existing rockets to place a huge spacecraft into a high orbit. A spacecraft that expanded or deployed parts of itself. This created the improbable probe seen in the photograph taken by the black satellite. They may have specifically designed this probe to look 'alien'. The command platform to control their probe might still be up there, in a very high orbit.

The other side has focused on keeping that platform hidden. That made it appear possible that someone or something somewhere else might have launched the probe. The platform is likely in an orbit designed to make it as difficult as possible to find. The probe might have flown to and somehow 'docked' with this platform when it disappeared. This was done to prevent the masquerade from being found out. But that would be another technology beyond the only superpower. And so, it is unlikely at best.

Regardless of the facts, the Empire's only possible course of action now is clearly war.

34 THROUGH A LOOKING GLASS

Everyone is reading all about it. Not just in the most powerful nation, the one that launched the probe on its mission of discovery, but everywhere. People all around the world are reading about it and seeing it for themselves. They have released photographs of the sister planet on the far side of the sun to the world Press. Now all can see that their world is not alone. There is a civilization on another planet. On the Other Planet right here in the neighborhood, as well.

The world holds its breath while talking a mile a minute for a couple of days. Then it heaves a collective sigh. For some it is a sigh of relief. Relief that we are not alone. There might be others to help show the way. For some it is a sigh of resignation. It's the realization of the sum of all fears. Interplanetary war could now be real. The Other Planet looks like it could come here just as the home world went there.

Governments form Committees and charter Investigations. They look into the consequences of a universe where God has sown life on multiple worlds. Some countries decide it cannot be real. They lock up the words and pictures and tell their citizens it is a hoax perpetrated by the Godless. It becomes a crime in these places to talk of the Other Planet. But not in the nation waging war halfway around the globe against a group of smaller nations. A group that stands in the way of peace and Security and resources.

The Leadership of the most powerful nation moves slowly at first. It forms a Committee to study the situation, but seems cautious in drawing conclusions. The triumvirate waits until other nations make Findings and adopt Action Plans. Some of those Plans include preparation for interplanetary war. Some declare Martial Law. And some call for implantation of microchips in all citizens. This is to prevent alien penetration. Finally, the most powerful nation acts in the reasoned and sensible manner befitting its place in the world.

The Leadership of the most powerful nation; the triumvirate of the Prime Minister, the Secretary of Security and War, and the President; declares an Extraordinary National Emergency or ENE. The ENE tightens Security at all levels of the government. It restricts entrance to the most powerful nation. And it postpones elections for the Leadership of the nation until further notice.

> These changes are necessary. They assure peace, Security, and continuity of leadership in these times of exceptional peril. Your government may make more changes later.

Almost all information that flows from the government to the people and private institutions that pay for it ceases. The government starts collecting every scrap of trivia about its citizens that it can find. Where there are no precedents for such prying, the government makes up new rules. These are based on broad interpretation of the already broad Patrician Act.

Government spies search people's library records and telephone records. Banks and credit bureaus open everyone's financial records to government browsing. They believe their 'big brother' will indemnify and reward them. The records are a tangle of irreconcilable data. So, all of the nation's credit agencies change their names yet again.

The government takes money from now quickly shrinking social programs. It uses the money to hire an undisclosed number of snoops. They perform new Department of Security and War operations.

Then they create a program called the Malevolent Activities by Nationals Inquiry and Eradication program. MEANIE will root out citizens who might be subject to coercion by aliens, home world or otherwise. MEANIE applies both in the country and abroad.

The traits of people vulnerable to coercion are many. They include questionable loyalty to the Federal government; involvement in minor religions or association with people from minor religions; sympathy for right to life or abortion rights groups; and membership in movements hostile to Federal rule. Groups hostile to Federal rule are for states' rights. They're also for labor unions, the liberal press, tax avoidance, and gun rights.

The government targets people with ethnic profiles that differ from those of the majority. But it does not admit to this – at first. And it targets people who object to this snooping and profiling. The government does this "— to preserve the peace and Security of our way of life."

The government encourages and then requires people to spy and report on their relatives and friends. 'Suspicion is Trust' proclaims a new screen saver. The screen saver comes free of charge as part of a Security download. The download is mandatory for the operating system that is employed by all of the nation's computers.

> To assure the Security of trusted citizens, the government will accept no new writs of habeas corpus. All pending writs are void.

The government may now choose to treat citizens as it does enemy soldiers held outside the country. They can hold citizens without charges or trial. And they can do it for as long as they want. The government can refuse to admit that it is holding you.

A new Federal Initiative outlaws some non mainstream religions. The Initiative goes by an already familiar acronym. Real churches applaud Choose The Right Church. The government crushes an upstart religion in the nation's West. The religion is known for its states' rights stance. And for its lax attitude toward male members with multiple wives.

> Consolidation under the real God's auspices is necessary.
> This sends a clear message about where this one nation

truly stands.

Congress approves a proposal to add the words 'Under God' anywhere they'll fit in the nation's Loyalty Oath to its flag. It just ignores the Constitution's ban on laws regarding the establishment of religion.

It defeats a proposal to include the word 'equality' in the Oath. The Oath's author, a socialist, wanted to include it long ago. But men worried, then as now, that they intend to apply 'equality' to people of other than the majority race, and to females. Congress ejects the sponsor of the Initiative from her seat.

Then it is Micah's turn. The arbitrary finger of fate that is crisscrossing the nation falls on him. It is obvious that Raven Winthrop is a traitor to the nation that gives her so much freedom. Micah supports this female in her Stand against the government. He has agreed to be married to her. The government revokes Micah Daegan's Exemption to Forced Sacrifice. It does this without any need for 'due process'.

And that is the beauty of the Patrician Act. The government just has to say a secret tribunal has determined it to be so. And it is. It isn't necessary to hold an actual hearing. No one can prove a secret trial hasn't taken place! Any Leadership apparatchik can just write down the desired finding and it is fact, destined to be history.

The only superpower uses small 'tactical' weapons of mass destruction on the other side of the world. It has decided to try something old, while hiding behind something new.

The Emperor makes a rare visit to the Junta's Nest. The Press quotes him on the escalation against those who will not acknowledge the only superpower's natural rights.

This deployment will shorten the war and save lives on both sides.

"A God expresses concern that this struggle has gone on so long," says the news. "He offers a final solution to minimize the costs of securing the nation's life blood. Our Emperor cares greatly for those in his charge. He steps in when the Commander in Chief and Junta are having difficulties. He lights the way for us all."

The other side on the superpower's world also has need of life's blood. They cannot allow the superpower to control it all and strangle their development. 'They' includes several nations besides the large one the superpower tells its citizens they should fear and hate. And They conspire to test the superpower's resolve – and its 'impenetrable' shield.

In a small, obscure Republic half way around the world from the superpower a space launch occurs. One of the superpower's black satellites detects the launch. It does so just as the rocket completes its 'boost phase'. After the engines burn out, the payload enters space to cruise silently on. And the spent upper stage falls back into the atmosphere.

Computers near the War Room in the superpower's enormous six-sided command complex in the capitol go to work. They calculate the path and possible impact zones of the unknown payload. The accuracy with which the payload's location and path are known increases twenty minutes later. A second satellite confirms and refines the trajectory. But it fails to determine the package's altitude.

Both observations have been due to one lucky break. The first satellite happened to be in the right place at the right time. It was easy to detect the launch then. The second black bird found the silently cruising vehicle. It was told where to look.

Twenty-five minutes have gone by since the launch. The payload is now less than twenty minutes from landfall. But its altitude is not known. It will impact somewhere along a known path across the superpower. Or it will go into orbit over it. And the only system capable of doing anything about it is SDS.

ALL WE ARE GIVEN

BOOK 12

Surprise, Surprise

ALL WE ARE GIVEN

35 A MOUSE ROARS

The only superpower in the universe and its Ruling Class know they have the biggest bombs. They know because they have monitored all the bomb tests the other side has performed over the years. The superpower has tested, both in the atmosphere and underground, much bigger bombs. And they have their dead and dying citizens downwind of the test site in the heartland of the nation to prove it.

What the superpower does not know is that there has been method to the other side's madness. Years ago, They, the other side, began testing much smaller weapons. The superpower's intelligence people were confused. But they finally decided that these were 'tactical' weapons. They are for use on an otherwise conventional battlefield.

These little bombs are not for a big exchange with the superpower. They are for little wars in Their own region of the planet. A Finding made at the time determined that this was a good thing.

"Let Them concentrate on whatever it is They are doing. We will keep building bigger and better bombs to use on Them at an appropriate time."

The MIRV weapons 'bus' is just reentering the atmosphere when the SDS birds acquire it. They establish that it is not in orbit and prepare to engage. The bus is tossing off Multiple

Independently-targeted Reentry Vehicles – small bombs – left and right. The SDS lasers begin firing. The bus is skipping about the outer edge of the atmosphere. It is using its own liquid fueled rocket engine. It is dodging fire, while throwing off ten individual bombs. And it deploys countermeasures designed to confuse defensive systems.

Two of the bombs escape the lasers but fail to function. They fall to break open on the ground. SDS hits and destroys five of them. Three functional weapons get by the impenetrable shield. Two of these hit the target – a large, sprawling coastal city. The ten little bombs were to blanket the city's shape. That would have destroyed it more completely than a single big weapon could.

Loss of life and property is enormous. The weapons that fell and broke open add to that. They become unintended 'dirty bombs'. They spread horrible slow death by radiation. A small Republic no one thought capable of such a thing has initiated a first strike on the only superpower in the universe. And on a lot of fish killed by the third functional but off-target weapon.

36 STRANGE LOVE

Citizens and some of the Press raise cries of "treason" and "betrayal" over postponement of the elections. Harsh retribution from the government quickly follows. The Secretary of Security and War invokes the Patrician Act's most onerous sections. These are the parts he promised would never be used against citizens. They separate protesters from liberty, and in some cases from life.

Some Press organizations still refuse to broadcast or print the official line. The government seizes them. They sell them off in pieces. They sell them to the vast media conglomerates that have supported this Leadership all along.

> Due to the war this free nation is forced to endure, all so-called civil liberties are suspended. The Government reserves for itself all authority to deal with insurrection and subversion. Without resort to public courts or review by any other entity.

This pet is more than fixed. They have pinned it down and dissected it. Like a frog just removed from the killing jar.

The government rewards the 'right' religions with official Federal status. They glory in dismembering the religions that have worshipped the wrong God or in the wrong ways. The government outlaws groups that claim there is no god. They find these groups' members lynched – murdered – in some places.

Micah has been lucky. Some secret court has found him guilty of subversion or sedition or some other charge. His conviction bars him from joining the military. He had not requested admission. But all males age sixteen years or more and without an Exemption are now Available. As defined by the new Federal Identification System for Tracking or FIST.

Females are now exempt from Military Service. They are also exempt from the minimum wage laws. Mass demotions and wage reductions for women follow. Finally, the nation's corporations have some relief from the high cost of labor. A cost they claim has kept them from competing in international markets. Repeal of the entire Federal minimum wage law will be considered later.

The Leadership hires nationally known Pet Control, Inc. They are to evaluate the use of implanted microchips for citizen identification.

"Miss Winthrop, you are free to go."

"Come with me, daughter. Let's get you home. This nightmare is over for you." Raven is in the room with two walls and two barred sides again. She doesn't know why. She hasn't seen any visitors in weeks. Raven is confused and disoriented when her father appears and leads her away. They go down a short corridor to the main circulation hall; through the heavily barred receiving station with its concrete and bullet-proof glass jailers' box in the center of the passage; and finally, out into free air and a waiting limousine.

"Are you alright, Raven?" asks Markus when the car is on its way out of the prison.

"I think so, Daddy. I need sleep. It will be wonderful — in my own bed. The drugs — in my food are still making me groggy. But that's — not sleeping. I'm so tired. Forgive me — I'm sorry — I keep falling partly back into a dream. I've been having it — the dream — for the longest time. For days now. I think."

"The Other Side is making a big show in the Press over your release, Raven," says Markus. "In their Press that is. They now have absolute control of all the officially sanctioned media. The Leadership claims that keeping women from participating in the military is 'natural law'. They argue that doing otherwise leads to breakdowns. Such as the one they claim you've had. They're trying to commandeer your ordeal. The one they put you through. To prove their position that females should not have the same responsibilities as males.

"It appears that leads to other 'natural' conclusions," continues Markus. "Paying women sweatshop wages being the first. I shouldn't be surprised to find shortly that there is no reason for women to worry themselves with voting for the men who will represent their interests.

"You've been released as a show of good will, Raven. You were 'legally imprisoned for violating a valid law at the time'. But that law is no longer on the books. They have commuted your sentence to time served. And all this without a trial that we know of! You're expected to be grateful, my dear. We both know you're a lot smarter than that."

37 STALEMATE

The only superpower in the universe hesitates. The Ruling Class hadn't planned on a full-scale exchange with Them at this time. It dismays the superpower that their impenetrable shield is only as good as old analyses told them it would be. Analyses done before they fielded the SDS hardware. Fifty percent effective in the field on first use is not a bad number for complex military systems. It stinks as a predictor of friendly casualties in an all-out global war.

Forty percent of the bombs that made it through the shield were direct hits. The small Republic's success rate, past the shield, is about what was predicted. The overall success rate for Their ten little bombs, thirty percent detonating in or next to the target zone, is just within the old benchmarks. Those old estimates don't consider the superpower's expensive new shield. And then there is the dirty bombs bonus.

Their achievement emboldens Them. But They do not follow-up. Both sides are aware of another analysis. One that concludes too many bombs going off at once makes for a long hard 'winter'. Once again both sides know that they are vulnerable.

The results of the mid-level elections are not what the Leadership forecast. They are not what the Other Side hoped for either. The loyal opposition wins a small majority in the national legislature for the first time in a long time. It is not enough to turn the tide.

"Damn," says Representative Winthrop, putting down his newspaper. "The President has made good on his threat to veto my bill rescinding the new Armed Forces Commissions Act."

"What's that, Daddy?" asks Raven.

Markus, Nancy, Raven, and Micah are sitting in the Winthrops breakfast nook having lunch. Micah has been a regular visitor to the Winthrops' home since Raven was released from prison. He's beginning to feel like a member of the family.

"It's a companion law to the Patrician Act," replies Markus. "It sets up more secret courts. Courts that are supposed to be for trials of people the government is holding outside the country."

"It's another nail in the coffin of freedom," says Micah. "The underground paper I pick up on campus says it flies in the face of the Constitution's guarantee of public trials. It erodes the right to defend against unjust charges."

"When you return to school next year, you'll find that paper is no longer available," says Markus. "The Leadership says that trials under the Commissions Act of people they label 'enemy combatants' are protected. They're protected from disclosure, even to the Legislature. They say it's a matter of national Security.

"And now they say that MEANIE trials of citizens are protected too. They base these claims on powers granted them under the ENE declaration. And on parts of the Patrician Act."

"But, Dad, how can they get away with that? The people and the Press won't allow it!" says Raven.

"I'm afraid, daughter, that the people have been frightened into going along. The Leadership has told them that it's just temporary. That it's a small price to pay to keep outside forces from destroying our country. And the Press has ceased to be independent. Like the banks, they now owe their allegiance only to their big brother, the Federal government.

"Now the triumvirate says that the Legislature can't reclaim their constitutional powers. Powers that the prior Legislature gave away in a panic. There are not enough new Legislators to override Presidential vetoes. The President is vetoing laws that we passed to return the country to democracy."

The PM and the Secretary of Security and War play the Fear Card. They play the Fear Card repeatedly. They appeal to the people's fear of threats from outside the country. These two men know that adding fear to the formula encourages the process to proceed.

> This is a time of war and assaults on our way of life from all sides. Anyone who argues against efforts by the Leadership to assure Security and peace must be our enemies.

Fanatics commit acts of terror against their own citizens in the countries that threaten Security and peace and access to resources. These acts just appall voters in the most powerful nation. But terrorism directed across the sea at these same voters drives them nearly to hysteria. And yet, for some reason, they cannot imagine treason from within stealing their freedom.

Voters support the triumvirate's harsh methods 'over there'. But they expect the same Leadership to voluntarily return to the rule of law here. It seems that "The only thing necessary for the triumph of evil is for good men to do nothing" to prevent it. Or for people to see it as an inherent difference between Them and Us.

38 ALL WE ARE GIVEN

Something must be done. People in the most powerful nation can feel their privacy, their families' safety, and their freedom to know and participate slipping away. This happens in the name of some vague and external 'Security'. The new laws that do this are clearly in violation of the Constitution of the land. The triumvirate and their advisors are driving this rush to dissolve liberty. The rest of the government is simply shrugging and signing on.

There are a few exceptions to this surrender. These are usually people from the Other Side. The Leadership's Party is ejecting legislators from important posts if they oppose the changes. The opposition knows that this may mean losing the larger fight to stop the slide into despotism. So, many take the easier and 'better overall' strategy of complaining vocally; while voting sheepishly, for now, with the Leadership's Party.

Markus Winthrop, Esquire is one who refuses to go along. He helps organize and participates in the caucuses of Legislators who are concerned by the new laws. These meetings include some lawmakers from the Leadership's own Party.

Markus sponsored the successful bill to repeal the Commissions Act. But the President's vetoed it. There are not enough votes to override the President. Only Representative Winthrop's stature in the capitol and in his important home state have saved him. They prevented the same Leadership response to

Markus Winthrop as befell the woman who wanted to add the word 'equality' to the Oath.

Raven knows it will fall to her in the end. She feels it in her soul. Someone must do something right here, and soon. Raven knows that her 'religion', her desire to serve her fellow beings and care for her world, will drive her to action. She can count on Markus, Nancy, and Micah to help. But it will be up to her to actually do something. Raven is frightened by her growing resolve. But, like all heroes, she moves beyond her fear and steels herself for action. But: what action?

How can a woman many will still count a girl challenge the system? Can a new Arts and Letters graduate step into the charged atmosphere of a nation in crisis and make a difference? How will she help preserve the country's freedom? What chance has she, when good women and men across the land are failing to stop this wall of cunning deceit, cold indifference, and lockstep mindlessness?

Raven knows this time – right now – is her time. She has just burst on the public stage. She has the name recognition to grab people's attention well beyond the Capitol and the Winthrops' home state.

"What can I offer that can help turn the tide?" Raven thinks. "Do I have anything at all?

"All I have is what I am. What I believe to be right and true. What I hope to do with my own life is what I have to bring to this fight." And that is all any of us are truly given.

"It will have to do. But, how do I use it?" Raven knows that when tyrants tell you to shut up and take it – live as they demand, under their yoke – they are telling you to die. They want you, as a thinking person, to cease to be. Either you literally die or you give up your free will and maybe even your awareness. You become part of the surplus population they consider it their right to savage. It's all the same to oppressors. You're meat for the grinder either way.

If you won't be a sheep – a pet subject to its Prince's whims – then you must cease to be. Sheep have been told all their lives that obeying without question is patriotism. Nothing could be further from the truth. But Raven knows that some have chosen to be sheep. These moral cowards must always side with their masters to validate that decision. They must disregard reality and logic to recite again and again the official lies.

"Even Princes' 'attack dogs' are often only sheep in wolves' clothing," thinks Raven.

"I must try to reach everyone," she realizes. "What I do must persuade both patriots ready to defend their country from would-be despots and those who are confused. I must wake those that have been taught not to think. I must show those who choose not to think, that things more important than their lazy cowardice hang in this balance. This threatens the very lives of their children and grandchildren. And if I could reach beyond this land, to the rest of the world including our allies now recoiling from what we are becoming; well, that might help too."

"I didn't think I'd see this day, Ibrahim. At least, not so soon after the completion of SDS. I wish you well out there."

"Thank you, Neil. You should know that you gave me the inspiration to leave SDS Support and Logistics Services. Your example made me realize I would be missing life if I were to forgo having a family for my career. That is why I am not going to work for any program to militarize space beyond our current systems.

"The destruction of our great western city and the standoff with the Eastern Empire have made me understand what a failure SDS was destined to be," says Ibrahim. "That is not the way.

"I have been seeing your wife's friend. The woman you introduced me to during your god's festival. Do not be too surprised if you receive an invitation to a wedding.

"Of course, it may be too late for us. I intend to live as much as possible before the end of my time, and perhaps of all time. I will leave hate behind and try something new. Something only talked of before in the world's history. I will live that which has been imagined by 'dreamers and fools'. But rejected as impossibly naïve by the ultimate fools. Those who persuade us all to forego life in the pursuit of death.

"I have secured a position in a program for space exploration," continues Ibrahim. "It does not pay as well in dollars. And the job is unsure as to longevity. But it's a reason for life and not a reason for death. It is something I can be proud to tell my children of in the future. If any of us have a future. I do not believe what I have done up to now to be something to be proud of."

"What is this 'space exploration', Ibrahim?" says Neil.

"It has come about because of those space rocks that changed our planet's life forms and the world's path," replies Ibrahim. "Our lack of knowledge of the universe outside the tiny space around us – from our low orbit spies to our high orbit defenses – is a mistake. Even those who rule admit that now. We must know more about our universe. That is our only chance to prevent our destinies being changed by a random event from on high.

"We have a bit of money to build the first true spacecraft. These will be machines of exploration and discovery instead of death. Our first goal is to orbit and investigate our moon. There will be more and greater goals in the future."

"Someone or something is capable of more, Ibrahim," says Neil. The probe that did not exist and did not orbit our world was beyond what you have described. The way it changed its orbit; its size and the materials it was made of; and its launch from somewhere other than the planet – all of these are beyond our capabilities. Aim for that level of ability, my friend, and your new Endeavour will carry you beyond the moon."

"What of you, Neil? asks Ibrahim. "Will you stay and continue servicing the system you helped to build because you believe it is a necessary evil?"

"I will. I do so now to protect my children," says Neil. "If global war comes, as our leaders seem determined to have it; perhaps SDS will protect the city or cities where my children live. Many will not be saved. But there is that fifty percent chance the system will be effective. Here, or wherever my children are living then.

"And there is renewed talk of upgrading SDS. If we insist on living only to kill our fellow beings; we must also prepare to defend against their striking back at us. As they surely must and will."

BOOK 13

The End

39 OF FUTURE'S PAST

Both Dr. Mariam and Jenny Daegan have been expecting their formal invitations for some time. The world is about to reach a major space milestone. It has been nearly fifty years since the first artificial satellite orbited the globe. This is an important anniversary for the most powerful nation. And the Leadership wants to make the celebration important for the entire world.

One of the largest media networks has been assembling a lavish show for the airwaves. They first contacted Dr. Baker and Representative Daegan a year ago about participating. The show will be a moderated discussion of the past and the future of space exploration. They will broadcast both television and radio versions. So that even backwaters of the planet can tune in. The telecast will include photos and videos of space firsts. Works of art will depict the future of discovery and exploration.

Space Launch Complex One's legendary Launch Director, Dr. Mariam Baker, will be an honored guest on the show. She will narrate parts of the program. The Chairman of the National Space Exploration Committee will be a moderator. Representative Daegan's Party expects her to show their Leadership in a flattering light. They want to be seen as supportive of NSEA's long-term goals. And as backers of the President's Initiative for new crewed space exploration.

Space celebrities and officials from the most powerful nation and from other space faring nations will appear. Some of them will sit on the panel of moderators. The moderators will guide the program. They will question the heroes. They will take some questions over the Internet too. Artists, computer illustrators, and film and video makers from around the globe have submitted works. These depict their visions of new worlds. And views of the cosmos not yet seen. The televised program will showcase the best of these.

Jenny watches them make the prerecorded portions of the program. She sees the preparations for the live broadcast. It reminds her of waiting for a long-anticipated date for the prom or the premier of a new play or opera.

"Many preparations have been made. People are checking and rechecking to make sure those are just right. And everyone is expecting a perfect performance," she thinks. Rehearsals begin at last.

"Please, Miss, just let us climb up in there and get it down."

"It's mine, you know. Do you think I'd casually damage it or allow something to happen?"

"But it's our responsibility now. We have a contract and protecting it while it's with us is part of that. The Director's instructions were quite clear. He isn't keen on this secondary loan. Even if it is for a short time. It's our jobs on the line if anything happens. There is talk about making it part of the permanent collection. The Director thinks it may well be ours soon."

"And that will be up to me," says Raven. "I'm not sure I'm willing to part with it at any price."

The workers remove Raven's masterpiece from the van. It wears a new museum frame with a little silver sign proclaiming it 'Futures Repast'. They expertly maneuver it through the chaos on the large loading dock. It makes it into the Studio's prop room without incident.

Micah was embarrassed by the scene at the van. He understands Raven's obsession with her art. And he relates to her need to protect her work. But he would have allowed the deliverymen, trusted museum employees with their jobs on the line, to work without interference.

His embarrassment vanishes when he looks around the prop room at the pieces for the show. Micah is proud of Raven. He is proud of her art. He recognizes how unique and exceptional her passion and skills are.

"My mother is here somewhere," says Micah. "Now that the live presentation is close, she's spending a lot of time rehearsing."

"Even my father has been working on this," replies Raven. "He's the chair of the committee preparing for the opposition's participation. Markus says the only man from our Party that the Leadership will allow onstage is a milquetoast. Someone who will say only what he's told to. He won't volunteer anything that might sound political."

"It's about perception," says Micah. "It wouldn't do to have something said on the air that suggests other than devotion by the triumvirate to exploration for the sake of knowledge. We will eventually see the Leadership's true motives in arranging this program and proposing new crewed space missions.

"This show is costing more than all the Leadership has done so far to put us on the path to new knowledge. The President's Initiative reduces the money spent on science while increasing money for new flight hardware. We may be going farther sometime in the future. But we won't be bothering with basic research when we do."

40 THE GULAG

After Raven recovered from her ordeal in the Leadership's prison, she and Micah considered what to do with their lives. The only thing known for sure is that they want to spend their lives together.

Micah was horrified when he heard the details of Raven's time behind bars. She faced sleep deprivation, forced drugging, and solitary confinement. This was how the Leadership punished a young woman accused but not convicted of having a mind. Micah knows it would still be going on if not for the triumvirate's demotion of women to a lower class of citizenship.

"I think we should consider having our wedding, and our life together, in another land," Micah says. But Raven will not have it. She made the decision a long time ago in her short life. She will Stand right here and fight for what she believes in.

Both Raven and Micah had privileged childhoods. The harsh realities of the real world then seemed otherworldly. But now Raven has had radical thoughts and violent actions directed against her. These were not the ideas of 'radical college professors'. They were the real radicalism and violence of ideologue politicians. And of their rabid religious followers.

The experience has changed an intelligent but naïve young woman. Raven was an artist who wanted only to make the world a more harmonious place. The people who tried to make her into a mindless sheep changed her into a passionate reformer. Raven sees where her convictions must now lead her. Micah understands this only on an intellectual level.

Micah isn't a coward. But he was taught from childhood to avoid confrontation. He is like those taught that submission to authority, right or wrong, is patriotism. When nothing could be further from the truth. Micah hasn't learned the difference between rash confrontation and defense of inalienable rights.

Truth and freedom often require forceful and even fierce defense. Sometimes that fight is against outside enemies. But sometimes it is against those who would destroy freedom from within. And often peace and Security must take a back seat to freedom.

"Dear, leaving the country to escape this oppression would be like allowing the bastards to put me back into their gulag," says Raven. "They have scattered their secret political prisons around the world. They hide them from people deluded in thinking themselves still free. We cannot leave our own nation behind to reclaim our freedom. That would remove the proof on this soil that things have been reversed. That freedom does not ring here anymore."

Micah makes the leap to understanding. He pledges his life and honor to the struggle to return freedom to his country. But it isn't his own life Micah is thinking about as he still considers fleeing. Raven recently told him there are now two young lives he cares deeply for. And which are at risk here.

41 A LIGHTER SHADE

Panels of historians recommended the topics to include. Art directors, authorities, and esteemed artists; the illuminati of photography, video and film, music, painting, and sculpture; selected the finalists. Lastly, the artists whose works they chose were investigated. To assure that no agendas or politics they might express can taint the program.

The words, videos, and art works will describe the past and future of space exploration. They are to offer "— an historically factual and logically forecast account of discovery." They will celebrate the lives of those who contributed and those who are still contributing. Some of these people will be in attendance. There will be only necessary references to nations or politics. The show is to treat the guests as one family of explorers.

Futures Repast is a gem in the collection. It is currently on loan to Capitol Art Museum. The museum's permanent collection will likely acquire it. Investigators scrutinize R. M. Winthrop. They want to know her politics and other critical characteristics.

Raven has an engaging personality. She comes with the proper genetic background, the majority profile. She has a proper social standing including church affiliation. She has name recognition due to events in the news and her father's position. Raven has been positioned for greatness.

The Leadership has judged Raven "a victim of the liberal

press and radical college professors." She has "— suffered due to improper pressures and ideologies forced on a young woman." The triumvirate pardoned Raven for her recent descent into madness. They decide that her case does not require another full review at this time. A check shows no recent deviant behavior.

Futures Repast tells the story of two cultures coming together in peace over a shared meal. One group appears more advanced than the other. There are flying machines landing at the edge of a large natural clearing in a wood. It is a meadow in glorious spring bloom. A seemingly primitive people serve food to all on roughhewn tables in the foreground. Hunched-over figures tend to crops on farmed land to one side of the meadow.

The contrast in the two groups' clothing is striking. One group wear clothes made from nature. The others' clothes have been slickly manufactured.

The two groups' skins are different colors. The shapes of their eyes and other features are not the same. The advanced people have markings that run up both sides of their necks. These double lines of irregularly shaped spots disappear into their hair behind their ears. These are similar but not identical to Raven's own beauty lines.

The people are gesturing – signing – to communicate. Some are seated and eating. Some are standing. One gestures to the horizon. Others point to the meadow and the crops, or to the silvery machines. It is twilight. Two moons are arrayed in the sky. That sky darkens to black at the top of the canvas. A few brightest stars shine out. Whether this is a reunion or a first contact is unstated. It is clearly a meeting of warmth and peace.

42 LEAP OF FAITH

They chose Raven's masterpiece as the finale to the program. It is the finest, most inspiring work foretelling accomplishment and hope for the future. They asked R. M. Winthrop to record a description of her painting for the radio audience. They asked her to pen her vision of the future. A future where people might communicate with intelligent creatures on far off planets.

The night of the live broadcast arrives with high expectations for that perfect performance. People check every detail one last time. Everything seems to be coming off as planned. There is a substitution for the Representative from the Other Side. The cast and stagehands all recognize him. He is the missing man's coach. He likely knows the program as well or better than the ill Representative.

The evening begins as a history lesson. In the background are blown-up still photos of the Other Planet. Its cities glitter through the perfect black of space to outline the coasts of unknown continents. The radio program uses a voice behind the main narration to also convey this newest news. The main tracks of both programs trace the development of space vehicles. They begin with that first tiny satellite. That was launched half a century ago. They applaud the first space explorers.

The show introduces Dr. Mariam Baker early on. The name of the legendary Launch Director of Space Launch Complex One is known around the planet. Dr. Baker has never designed or piloted a spacecraft. But they treat her as one of the heroes on this occasion. 'Dr. Mariam' appears in the videos more and more frequently as the program catches up in time to today.

"The sole purpose of our programs to explore the planets, moons, and stars is scientific knowledge," says Dr. Baker. She is beginning her live presentation. "Only by reaching out to measure, record, and touch the cosmos can we truly understand this universe we are a part of. Social science – knowledge of ourselves, our relationships, and our institutions – is part of the fabric of our understanding. Natural science strives just to provide knowledge of the universe in which we live. It is a rigorous and objective tool for measuring reality. Its discoveries and data must be independent of policies and agendas of any kind.

"Those who would alter or hide science's findings, in the name of politics or religion, are enemies of both freedom and knowledge. They are terrorists. As are those who would destroy our facilities and kill our scientists. We must never allow those things to happen.

"Today we celebrate our successes and what we have learned from our failures," she continues. "The men and women who choose to give their lives to this Endeavour of truth are heroes of the planet. Their sacrifices have helped us move away from the dark past of superstition. And toward new understanding for all.

"Here is what our science, our technology, and our exploration have brought us," says Mariam. She waves to the background photos. They are brought forward dramatically in the video. The camera pans a long line of shots of the improbable probe. The still photos show its launch and transformation. The probe's acceleration past the big moon and journey around the sun go by. And finally, it arrives in orbit at the sister planet.

"Each culture sees both its past and its future in the other," says Raven. She has just described the composition, colors, and mood of her masterpiece. "One people stand on the edge of the ocean of the universe and the other only on the edge of tilled soil. But there is a common leap which binds them. That leap gives each the possibility of a bright future. Both have stood up from a savage past to an idea which is the only answer of life.

"It is not an easy leap to make. Many people want to hold back those who try. Those who attempt the jump must do so in strength and not in fear. The time must be ripe on each world for the attempt.

Another thing these people share is knowledge of the struggle to get here. It seems for one it was a journey across the heavens and for the other only across a meadow. But the struggle for both has been more complex than that – and more personal.

"We have seen dark times on our own world," Raven continues. "Times when people forgot their way and stepped back to savagery. We lost the social and natural knowledge of hundreds and even thousands of hard-fought years. We have experienced times so dark that our histories label them that.

"We cannot allow that to happen again – ever. The time is ripe on our world for the next leap. We must cast off the past of superstition and creed. No one has the answers for all. Those who would kill our bodies or our minds to enforce their personal 'truths' must be resisted with all our might. We must relegate those ideas and methods to the dark ages of our past. If we are ever to live in the light.

"All on our world may not be ready for this future. They will arrive there in their own ways and times," continues Raven. "We can help, but not by force. That can only drag us backward. We cannot demand that our citizens mindlessly obey. That is a return to darkness. We can and must protect ourselves. But we must not do that with cunning lies and secret laws. Anything we do that is hostile to the freedom and informed consent of the governed is failure. And those who say otherwise are relics of a past to which we must just say 'no'."

"We thank you, Miss Winthrop, for your presentation," says Jenny. "We thank you too for your vision in Futures Repast of a bright prospect for our species. And for all who commit to life rather than death.

"I hold it true that we must voyage across this final frontier, the infinity of space, with a willingness to embrace those different than ourselves. The constants that I think we will find among enlightened species are commitments to life rather than death; and to truth – to individual freedom and responsibility."

"I sincerely affirm these self-evident truths in the name of the Other Side of the House of Representatives of my great country," adds Markus Winthrop. "I believe that however far we go, we will find ourselves there looking back at us. Ourselves with all our fears and failures, and with all of our aspirations and noble hopes for a greater and more inclusive future."

"That concludes tonight's program," says the narrator. "Those who missed part of the show or who wish to view or hear it again in its entirety should tune in these same two hours tomorrow. Times and dates will vary. Good day and good night."

The red lights on the cameras go out. The Director gives the signal that they are off the air. Then all hell breaks loose.

The presentation by R. M. Winthrop and concluding remarks by two panelists took seven minutes. Raven's father, a powerful leader of the opposition in the House, spoke last. But all he did was second the words of the Leadership's own Representative Daegan. No one saw it coming.

They had screened Miss Winthrop's descriptions of her painting and her vision for political content. It only became apparent in the last part of her speech. Raven deviated only slightly from what she had written.

The programs have been broadcast. People and nations all around the planet have recorded them. Broadcasters everywhere have scheduled these for repeat "— in these same two hours tomorrow." That depends on where you ask. The triumvirate will not be pleased.

All Raven did was describe Futures Repast. She put into her own words the ideals it depicts. No one wants a future where we communicate with creatures on far planets to include a narration like "And deceive them into thinking we are friends. While we make plans to exterminate them." Even the Prime Minister likely does not want that narrative.

Raven did not provide cover for the big lies. For the actions exactly opposite words and promises. These are the daily stock of this Leadership's rule. Unlike a good sheep, she offered no defense for the masters. She stepped aside. She allowed the Leadership's actions and policies of hate and exclusion to stand clearly exposed by the light. Raven let the triumvirate hang themselves.

Motherland Security tried to stop Raven as she reluctantly walked away from her masterpiece. Representative Winthrop stepped in. He told the men that his daughter needed rest. If they must, they should contact her at home later. Even Motherland Security wavered when they faced Markus's eminence.

Jenny used the crowd of reporters and well wishers that enveloped her as cover to reach a nearby exit. She left the uniformed men who tried to approach her lost in the crowd. Micah was waiting for all of them. He drove a borrowed car as fast as he dared, without attracting Agents, to the Representatives Chambers Building.

A parliamentary maneuver was taking place on the Chamber floor when they arrived. It was about a Resolution that had bounced about the House of Representatives for weeks. It had few sponsors and little chance to come to a vote. Given the late hour, there were a lot of Legislators and others here.

The morning newspapers said that a key lawmaker, a leader of the opposition, added his name to the list of the Resolution's sponsors. Some Legislators from the Leadership's own Party then added their names to the list. Some said there might be a vote on the Resolution.

Representative Winthrop slowed to survey the scene as they walked past open doors to the Chamber floor. More than a few people inside raised their hands in greeting. Raven, Micah, and Jenny joined the rest of Markus's family and Jenny's husband in Representative Winthrop's private offices.

The President canceled the second broadcast of The History and Future of Space Exploration. They didn't show it again in the most powerful nation. But it was shown again almost everywhere else around the world. Except where it's illegal to talk about the Other Planet.

The Resolution did come to a vote. It led to Articles of Impeachment against the PM and the Secretary of Security and War. These were amended to charge only the PM after the Secretary resigned.

It turned out that the small majority the opposition won in the midlevel elections was able to do something. The President tried to do it. But he had no Constitutional authority to veto Impeachment. A resounding override vote made that clear even to him.

The Prime Minister argued that he wasn't part of the system.

So, he wasn't subject to the law. This fell on deaf ears. The People finally had the last word.

It took about two months to begin winding down the war halfway around the globe. The fugitives had to remain hidden in Markus's offices only the first few weeks of that.

The President withdrew the plan to turn NSEA into the National Space Expeditionary Army. They rescheduled the elections. They were held on time, more or less. A full return to democracy took longer.

Raven's dream ended when Capitol Art Museum retrieved her masterpiece. They relocated it to its permanent new home on their walls.

And the President continues playing the Golf Card – in his retirement.

ABOUT THE AUTHOR

C. W. (Will) Crowther is an aerospace and nuclear engineer who worked on ICBMs, space launchers, and space shuttle Endeavour. He returned to school to study architecture. He has recently been an architectural designer and a construction project manager.

Will and his wife live in Salt Lake City, Utah, U. S. They have one son. Will also designs and makes furniture, sculpture, and graphic art.

ALL WE ARE GIVEN